CHEERLEADERS

#3

RUMORS

CAROLINE B. COONEY

SCHOLASTIC INC.
New York Toronto London Auckland Sydney Tokyo

ISBN 0-590-33404-2

12 11 10 9 8 7 6 5 4 3 2   5 6 7 8 9/8 0/9

Printed in the USA   01

CHEERLEADERS

RUMORS

CHEERLEADERS

CHAPTER

1

The six cheerleaders made a bright scarlet and white line against the gymnasium wall. Leading a rhythmic yell, they clapped steadily, slowly drawing the attention of the crowd to their corner of the gym. Olivia Evans, the youngest and least sociable of the Varsity Squad, hung back to glance into the boys' locker room. The captain of the basketball team, jogging in place, nodded at her.

"Okay," Olivia whispered to Mary Ellen Kirkwood, captain of the cheerleading squad. "Team's lined up."

Walt and Pres, the two boys on the squad, shifted position. Gripping an enormous wooden hoop to which a huge sheet of paper had been stapled, they stood blocking the entrance to the boys' locker room. The crowd, knowing that their team was about to appear, began stomping and clapping with wild abandon.

1

It was the moment Nancy Goldstein loved most in cheerleading: the building excitement, the shivering floor as fans pounded their feet on the risers, the raw nerves and fearful anticipation — *Will we win?*

It was the first basketball game of the season against Garrison High, Tarenton's arch rival, and excitement was at a fever pitch. There must have been four hundred people from Tarenton, and at least two hundred who had come by bus and car to see Garrison play.

The Tarenton cheerleaders were a breathtaking sight: the four Varsity girls, with Olivia at the end doing her astonishing gymnastic feats, the white pleats of their scarlet uniforms flashing, and the two muscular, handsome boys who made their squad such a special one.

Mary Ellen drew a deep breath, gearing herself up for the game ahead. "Fever cheer, squad," she directed. "And, go!" At the top of her lungs she yelled to set the rhythm, "Got *spirit?* Let's *hear it!*"

The boys held the hoop tightly, and with the girls they shouted:

> We've got the fever!
> We've got the *beat!*
> We're gonna give you
> A victory *treat!*

The captain of their basketball team burst through the paper hoop first and the others followed him. The cheerleaders screamed lustily as the crowd got to its feet (at least the Tarenton half of the crowd!) and yelled for Tarenton's best.

And the action began.

Tarenton had the kind of rivalry with Garrison that meant excited crowds. The cheer was no exaggeration — the fans *were* feverish. There were police around in case the excitement became violent, and the high school principal and vice-principals circulated tensely, keeping an eye on those likely to start something should they disagree with the referees. The fans, wanting to hear and participate in their own favorite cheers, yelled suggestions at the squad. Mary Ellen, who decided what cheers to use, was aware of nothing but the game. She cheered as though basketball was the core of her life — and on nights like this, it was.

Mary Ellen loved sports. Most of all she loved her own sport, cheerleading. She had a beautiful, lissome body, which she displayed joyously, the impressive full C jumps and the eye-catching pikes thrilling her as much as they thrilled the crowd that watched. Mary Ellen loved the attention that cheerleading brought her — from the crowd, from the boys on the team, and from the younger girls in school (including her own little sister) who idolized her.

She had a classic cheerleader image: golden girl with striking blue eyes, creamy skin, and long blonde hair. She wore her hair loose, but drawn away from a face that drew all eyes. Tonight, throwing herself with unparalleled enthusiasm

3

into the game, her hair fell from its carefully pinned position and bounced around her face, as if she were an innocent little girl of twelve.

The rest of the squad watched her out of the corners of their eyes, waiting for the next cheer cue.

"Pray for a time out," Angie Poletti murmured to Nancy. Nancy was new to cheerleading; it was only her second basketball game. Athletic and gymnastics-oriented as she was, Nancy had never been a cheerleader before. To have made Varsity on her first try was quite an honor. She didn't know all the ropes yet. "Why pray for a time out?" she asked Angie.

"Otherwise we'll never get to do anything but sideline cheers," Angie explained. "We won't have any real fun if we don't get out on the floor."

Across the gymnasium, the opposition team's cheerleaders were leading their fans in a similar cheer. A much more traditional squad than Tarenton, Garrison had a dozen girls in bright emerald green and white outfits. They were doing something new — moving in front of the risers in a diamond pattern. The Tarenton kids watched with interest because it was a cheer they might want to lift. Redo it a little, restructure it for their own unusual squad components — four girls and two boys.

Olivia whispered to Nancy, "Did you see that terrific outfit that Mary Ellen was wearing in school today?"

"*Yes!*" Nancy said. "Wasn't it gorgeous?

4

Mother and I were at Marnie's shopping and we saw it there, but Mother said it was too expensive for me to consider. Luscious fabric and colors. Looked so good on Mary Ellen with her fair skin, too."

But Olivia was not thinking of Mary Ellen's lovely features. She was thinking that Mary Ellen was poor. One of the poorest girls in school, grindingly poor compared to the rest of the squad members.

Nancy, on the other hand, had a father who was the head of a large accounting firm and a mother who was a part-time art history instructor at the community college. The Goldsteins lived in a lakefront house and had two fabulous cars. Think of Nancy's mother, then, saying that that outfit was too expensive. And yet Mary Ellen, who watched money so carefully that she didn't get a soda from the vending machine most of the time but brought juice in a thermos — Mary Ellen had that outfit on.

Olivia said musingly, "I can't figure out how Melon could afford that."

But Nancy, to whom money had never been an obstacle or a consideration, did not find this something worth talking about. She simply hoped that Mary Ellen had not heard Olivia use that hated nickname Melon. She said, "Hush. Mary Ellen's starting another cheer."

Gossiping, Olivia had almost missed seeing the terrific basket made by Troy Frederick, and it was her turn to do the congratulatory cheer. Nancy and Angie both nudged Olivia to get her started. Racing out on the sidelines, Olivia leaped into the air as only a tiny, lithe girl could — as though gravity had nothing to do with the human condition — and yelled, "Let's have a cheer for Troy! Yea, rah-hah, *Troy!*"

It was an indication of their coach's good work that even over the furor of such a huge crowd, you could still hear the piercing syllables of Olivia's cry. As she rose into the air, her short scarlet skirt lifted gaily, flouncing around her when she came down in a split. Olivia stayed in the split for several moments, enjoying its perfection. People who didn't know much about splits winced when she hit the floor, and people who did know how to do them were impressed, because for Olivia it all seemed so effortless.

Gracefully Olivia got up and trotted back to the squad, laughing all the way. Actually, laughter had not been part of Olivia's nature. She had led a grim life, with frequent operations and hospitalizations that had affected her mother even more than Olivia. The heart defects Olivia had as a child were long corrected, and she was as strong as any two ordinary girls. It was her mother, Mrs. Evans, who was permanently scarred with worry and followed her daughter around nervously, overprotecting her, fearful that something would go wrong again and her little girl would die young.

Under such circumstances, laughter was hard to come by. For Olivia, the hardest part of cheering was not the moves — she had taken years of gymnastics and fencing, and was far and away the most brilliant athlete of the six squad members — it was the constant required smile, so alien to her face.

She stood back in the Varsity line with the smile pasted to her lips and wondered about Mary Ellen. When cheering, the girls were allowed to wear no jewelry except earrings, and sometimes Ardith Engborg, their coach, prohibited those, too, if the earrings were too dangly or overly colorful. Mary Ellen had always worn plain gold studs — the same thick, dull studs put in the day her ears were pierced at the department store. But tonight she was wearing breathtakingly beautiful earrings that weren't from any discount jewelry counter. They were gold hearts laced together like a miniature fan, the center of each dotted with a tiny diamond.

Even if the diamonds are zircons, Olivia thought, those are definitely expensive earrings.

Patrick Henley got to the basketball game late. There wasn't a space in the bleachers that he could see as he gazed into the crowds. And definitely nothing in the seats behind the cheerleading squad, which was his preferred location. Watching Mary Ellen Kirkwood was his preferred occupation. Those of his friends he could spot were jammed so close together they couldn't squeeze in a strand of spaghetti, let alone the six feet and one hundred seventy pounds of Patrick Henley. All muscle, too. When you spend half the day hoisting heavy garbage cans and driving a truck, you don't stay skinny long. Patrick's father owned a garbage route, and Patrick proudly drove his own truck.

Patrick walked around the hall to come in on the other side of the gym. He disliked sitting with the opposite team's fans, but on the other hand he could now face the cheerleading squad across the floor and watch Mary Ellen. Patrick had spent his life watching Mary Ellen. Long before anybody else got in line to admire her, he was there. And though she resisted it, Mary Ellen adored him right back. She just made it painfully clear that she was not going to interrupt her game plan in order to fit a garbage man into her social life.

Patrick sighed. It was infuriating to adore Mary Ellen. He had tried year in and year out to break himself of the habit, but it was a little like giving up any other addiction — close to impossible. Well, they would both graduate from high school next year and that would end it all. He would stay in Tarenton, making a pile of money doing something that embarrassed her; and she would go off to New York and make a pile of money being a model.

Patrick was seventeen years old, and already buying his second truck. But he could not buy Mary Ellen.

As he watched her, he remembered how she felt in his arms. How she often resisted him, but then was unable to fight the never-ending desire there was between them. He knew the sweetness of her mouth and the softness of her arms around his neck.

The Tarenton squad was doing a complex line cheer, shifting way to the left in one kind of kick and then back to the right in another. Mary Ellen's golden body in the scarlet and white uniform was dazzling.

Troy Frederick, whom she was currently dating, made a free throw for Tarenton and Patrick almost forgot Mary Ellen in the excitement of evening up the score.

Mary Ellen sat herself down on the bench for a moment, getting her breath. She fingered her new earrings. She had beautiful hands: long, oval nails painted a ginger red. She stroked the tiny tendrils of yellow hair that lay on her cheeks. These earrings are too elegant for loose, flowing hair, she told herself. Loose hair is country girl. These earrings are sophisticated city woman.

Well, tonight, after the game, on her date with Troy, she would wear her hair in an elegant twist and then the earrings would be perfect.

Troy.

He was not Preston Tilford, III, but he was second best and she was ready to take him instead. Pres, one of the two boys on Varsity cheerleading, was the handsomest, richest boy in school. Mary Ellen had dated him on and off. She loved it all: loved riding in his Porsche, loved being seen on his arm, loved hearing her name linked with his in high school gossip.

But Pres Tilford was threatened by closeness. When he heard their two names linked, he backed off.

Both Pres and Mary Ellen put cheerleading

first. They were careful not to let their break-up (if you could break up with a boy you weren't actually going with) interfere with cheering. But it hurt Mary Ellen that Pres ignored her now. It hurt a lot, and covering the pain was difficult. And then Pres, instead of his usual social routine of a different girl every week, began seeing Vanessa, whom Mary Ellen hated. And that hurt even more.

But the hurt had eased with Troy's interest in her.

Troy was a year younger than Mary Ellen and exactly her height. She was so glad she had a new pair of flats to wear tonight.

Mary Ellen didn't often have new shoes. Just knowing they would slide on her feet, untouched, gleaming, was part of the excitement of the date to come.

She knew little about Troy, although he'd been going to Tarenton High for a year now. He was as rich as Pres, and lived next door to him, in a huge lakefront mansion built when the town first became a resort in the early 1900s. What his parents had done or presently did to acquire enough money to live on Fable Point, nobody knew. Troy's parents were the least visible adults in all of Tarenton.

In fact, Mary Ellen wasn't entirely sure that the two adults with whom Troy lived *were* his parents. She had a feeling there might have been so many remarriages that these were both unrelated stepparents. But Troy never discussed his family. If you really pressed him, he would be courteous, but his response would be about something else altogether, so the conversation would run something like this:

"Troy, what does your father do?"

"Basketball practice went pretty well today, didn't it?"

People tended to get the point and give Troy the privacy he demanded. Besides, he was an excellent basketball player — especially considering he was only five-nine — and good ballplayers, like good cheerleaders, could usually get their own way. Mary Ellen, to whom excellence was everything, could not bear to be seen with anybody who was not impressive. This attitude cut down considerably on the number of possible dates, and it also meant that the boy she *truly* yearned for — Patrick — was out of bounds.

Handsome, sweet, kind, and built as Patrick might be, he ran a garbage route. Mary Ellen was never going to date a boy who wanted nothing more than another garbage truck so he could expand his customer list, and she was never going to drive anywhere sitting on the passenger side of a garbage truck, so Patrick was *out*.

She touched her new earrings for the twentieth time that evening. Patrick doesn't go with these, she thought. Dreaming of Troy, watching him take the ball down the court, evading the expert defense of the Garrison team, she could even forget Patrick and concentrate on what suited her ends. Troy.

Because Troy would never talk about his personal life he never asked Mary Ellen about hers,

11

either. This was fine with Mary Ellen. She loved her family deeply, but she didn't love their jobs or income. A file clerk and a bus driver for parents? Who could brag about that? Who could find it even tolerable?

This would be her third date with Troy. He had not kissed her on the first two, much to her disappointment. Mary Ellen had been afraid he simply didn't want to and that she would never hear from him again. The relief at being asked out again was great. If Troy didn't kiss her tonight, maybe she would have to break the ice and kiss him first. It was worth thinking about!

The game, which began at eight, ended in screaming victory for Tarenton slightly after ten. Mary Ellen was glad because she was an intense fan and cared deeply about winning, but tonight she was especially glad. The team would go out to celebrate, and she would be Troy's date at the celebration. There was nothing worse than a basketball party after you'd *lost* the game. Might as well enjoy yourself at a funeral.

All the way into the locker room the departing cheerleaders yelled victory chants. Only one person in the bleachers stood still to watch them go . . . watched until the blonde girl with the cornflower blue eyes and the narrow ankles had vanished. Patrick Henley.

Mary Ellen showered slowly, happily, having perspired so much into her pullover that she had expected to drown in it. She who had to wear secondhand clothes, or buy irregulars in brand X jeans — *she* was finally the one in the best outfit. From Marnie's, no less. The loveliest, trendiest dress shop in Tarenton (which admittedly had very few trendy dress shops, or trendy anything, for that matter), but still — Marnie's! She touched the label, loving the whole idea of herself wearing clothing from Marnie's.

Slipping into the clothing excited Mary Ellen. The colors were muted rainbows, the fabric nubby and unusual. She was tall and slim enough to be able to carry off its baggy asymmetrical cut, and when she put it on she knew she looked as good as any model in *Vogue*. Which was, of course, what Mary Ellen planned to be in a few years: a topflight New York model. She brushed her hair vigorously, and then wove it swiftly into a twist of elegance.

Outside, parents left slowly, exchanging pleasantries with friends and neighbors. The numbers of people in the Tarenton High foyer diminished, but the sound level stayed high.

Preston Tilford, III, lounged in the shadow of the trophy case. He had not expected his parents to attend, and he was not disappointed or angry that he'd been proven right. When their son became a cheerleader, they faded away. Although Varsity cheering at Tarenton was athletic and demanding, and Pres was as macho a senior as Tarenton had, his father considered cheerleading for boys on a par with flower arranging or ballet. Every day for weeks his father had yelled at him: Pres should be using his energy working at the factory (the one Pres would one day inherit and run) at the loading

13

dock or some equally masculine location. Pres had ceased to argue with his father and the last several days had been relatively quiet at home. Perhaps his parents were merely gearing up for the next round. It was his mother's turn. Her style of fighting Pres was entirely different. She tried, and often succeeded, in making him feel guilty for failing her.

Pres's attention was removed from his parents for good when he heard a scrap of conversation not meant for his ears.

Inches away from him, two Garrison cheerleaders paused to shift their burdens of megaphone, pompons, overcoats, and handbags. If he had been wearing his own cheering uniform, they'd have recognized him, but in his navy blue sweater, faded jeans, and old sneakers, he was just a blond boy with his back to them.

One of them said softly, "I hear the captain of the Tarenton squad is a shoplifter."

Pres froze.

The other one squealed, "*Really?* You mean Mary Ellen Kirkwood? That beautiful blonde?"

"That's the one."

"Oh, how horrible. A shoplifter! Was she arrested? How can she still be on the squad? If *our* coach found out one of us was doing something criminal, we'd be off the squad in a split second."

"Listen," sniffed the first girl, "we'd get kicked off for having a beer, let alone shoplifting. But this is Tarenton. Anything goes. Crummy little

14

backwater town. Thank heavens my parents had sense enough to locate in Garrison."

The second one giggled. "Have they proved she's shoplifting?"

It was one thing for Pres to criticize Tarenton, another thing entirely for these twerps from Garrison to do it. And to insinuate that Mary Ellen shoplifted! Hypnotized by their topic, Pres walked right behind the two girls. If they turned around and saw who was following them, they'd be shocked right out of their sweaters. Pres and Walt were legends in their own time. In the entire state only five squads were coed, and Tarenton was the only one in this area. If the girls recognized Mary Ellen, they'd have Pres's fine features memorized.

"I guess it hasn't been proved," said the girl. "And I suppose it's innocent until proven guilty and all that. America, you know, and apple pie. Still, at a decent high school the administration would be looking into it."

"What can you expect from Tarenton?" said the other. She stopped to fish a Kleenex out of her purse. Pres felt like strangling her with her dangling scarf. "I bet they paid off the refs to get all those fouls called on our team. I never saw such a rigged game. It was disgusting. They didn't win. They were given the game by those rotten referees."

Pres stopped following them. He was getting too angry and there was no point in hearing more. What could he do, anyway? He could hardly beat them up. That wouldn't exactly restore his, Mary Ellen's, or Tarenton's honor. He couldn't demand a retraction. They'd just laugh.

The girls vanished into the Garrison team bus filled with their downhearted basketball players. Pres stood in the chilly night air, taking deep breaths cold enough to hurt. He drifted to the side of the building, where floodlights hit the hemlocks and made dark pools of midnight shadows. Moments later, Mary Ellen and Troy emerged from the school. Troy's arm was around Mary Ellen's slender waist. She looked ethereal: angelic and honey sweet.

Well, Pres had not dated Mary Ellen for long without finding that Mary Ellen was hardly either of those. But a shoplifter? Pres couldn't believe it. She was tough and she knew what she wanted. . . .

And she wants material things, he thought. She wanted me for my Porsche and my expensive dates. It was okay with me. I wanted her for her looks and figure. But *I* didn't buy her any jewelry. It wasn't that kind of thing between us. If she wanted it enough, would she —

It gave him a queer twist of disgust to imagine it.

Mary Ellen. Shoplifting.

He was deeply angry. Not that rage that skimmed the surface of his mind when he and his father argued, but rage he was ridden with, burdened with. Garrison cheerleaders had gotten hold of a rumor that he, Pres, had not heard on his own turf. No doubt it was the main topic in the Garrison team bus right now, spurred on by

16

the humiliation of losing the basketball game.

He could hear in his mind one of his mother's often repeated sayings: Where there's smoke, there's fire.

What would Troy's feeling be when he heard the rumor? For hear it he would. Rumors like that spread fast. Troy was Pres's next door neighbor, but he'd spent years in various boarding schools. Just why he was attending Tarenton High right now, Pres didn't know. By choice, as far as Pres could tell. But Troy so rarely committed himself to opinions, that Pres could only guess at what might be happening in Troy's home. Of all the boys Pres knew, Troy was one of the few who had not given (and was not *still* giving) Pres a hard time for having become a cheerleader.

Troy totally believed in the philosophy of live and let live.

Troy was right for Mary Ellen, Pres believed, because they were both such private people. They both so completely knew their own minds. A lot of the boys were threatened by Mary Ellen. The combination of her beauty, poise, and brains was a lot anyhow, but add to that her very strong will, and boys backed away as often as they drew close.

If Troy knew Mary Ellen was shoplifting, Pres thought, what would he do? Would he shrug? Cover for her? Drop her? Turn her in? He had a feeling that Troy would be unwilling to get involved one way or the other.

Pres went back in to find the crowds almost

17

gone. A few parents waited patiently; a lot more waited impatiently.

"Pres," said an irritable but sexy voice. "Pres, don't vanish like that."

Vanessa Barlow. He turned slowly to look at her. Vanessa was always worth looking at. If she weren't so conceited, if she'd tried harder last spring, she'd be on Varsity herself now. There were kids who'd expected Vanessa to get her father, the superintendent of schools, to put her on the squad by force. But Vanessa failed to make cheerleading by any method, and Pres had dealt with her bitter jealousy over and over.

Stunningly attractive, Vanessa had a habit of tossing her long, thick, dark hair so that it swirled sexily, and settled tantalizingly on her shoulders. Pres never saw Vanessa without wanting to take her hair in his hands and yank her toward him. She had a primitive personality, he reflected, which was probably part of the reason for his primitive response to her.

He had dated Vanessa when he stopped dating Mary Ellen. He felt Mary Ellen was crowding him, but he was not entirely sure what had drawn him to Vanessa. She wasn't a nice person, known through the high school for her tendency to be vicious to anyone in her path. But you never knew what to expect from Vanessa and there was a certain thrill to it, like driving the Porsche too fast down a road where there might well be a radar trap.

Tonight she looked pouty and sulky, the perfect expression for her tawny looks. "Are you

18

going to drive me home or do I have to go with my parents?" Vanessa asked. Her voice seemed to accuse him of various crimes.

Pres was not going home. There was a celebration party at Nancy Goldstein's. Nancy loved to give parties and her parents seemed to love them, too. Pres's mother disliked being a hostess for Pres; she was far too worried that her beautiful house would be wrecked by irresponsible teenagers. Her presence at a gathering was so dampening that Pres rarely brought his friends around.

But Mrs. Goldstein held the philosophy that she was happier having the kids where she knew exactly what was going on, and could be sure they had Pepsi and not beer, ginger ale and not booze. Only two games into the basketball season, Nancy had already given two parties.

Pres had offered to supply the soda this time. He had cases of it in the car.

He knew that Vanessa had heard about the party. He also knew that Vanessa, who had been exceptionally scheming and underhanded during tryouts and after, had alienated every one of the four girl cheerleaders and that Nancy would *never* invite Vanessa to her parties. Pres was still seething inside from the thoughts started by those Garrison girls, and he knew if he brought Vanessa, everybody would be tense.

His whole relationship with Vanessa was an irritable one. They snapped at each other, rather than exchanging endearments. He didn't need to be ashamed of his attitude because she responded in kind and thrived on it. Their relationship went

19

on in its hostile, sex-laden way without any ending.

"You're going to go home with your parents," he said, although he really felt like sitting in the Porsche with her and kissing her until she gave in. Just as well, really, that she had failed to make Varsity cheerleading. None of them could have worked with her on a daily basis.

Pres abandoned Vanessa, walking on down a darkened hall with no destination in mind. He had deliberately left her alone in public so that she would know he couldn't be bothered with her. But there was no pleasure tonight in having scored in their constant, undeclared war. Pres sighed and felt empty . . . felt abandoned himself.

The idea of Mary Ellen maybe being a thief, coupled with the demanding irritability of Vanessa, had upset him more than he'd thought.

Pres turned the corner in the hall and there near the drinking fountain were Andrew Poletti and his girlfriend Kerry Elliot, kissing.

Andrew's older sister Angie was a cheerleader with Pres. Andrew was younger than Angie by about ten months. A sophomore not good enough to be put in the basketball game unless it was the last twenty seconds and Tarenton was way ahead, Andrew mainly warmed the bench. Angie and Andrew were very close and often did things together, so Pres had run into Andrew and Kerry fairly often at cheerleading functions.

Kerry was slightly chubby, with thick, shapeless brown hair fluffed around her face and shoulders. She was the softest-looking girl Pres had ever seen: satin skin and pillowed hair.

He was brought to a stop by their kissing. Not the kind he and Vanessa indulged in. This was gentle. Cuddly. Affectionate.

Had Vanessa been there, she would have made cruel remarks about puppy love, fumbling inexperience, and so forth.

But Vanessa was not there, and what Pres saw was very sweet.

What am I, he thought — some sort of Peeping Tom? Keep walking, you jerk. Stop staring at them.

Suddenly Pres knew he had had enough of Vanessa. Let her be a tiger without him. Let her tantalize and irritate someone else. And he wasn't going back to Mary Ellen, either. Just who he would date he had no idea.

Pres glanced back at Andrew and Kerry. It was a fatal glance. Andrew had released Kerry and she was standing slightly apart from him, looking in Pres's direction, but not aware of Pres at all. She was the picture of sweetness and innocence.

And Pres — handsome, rich, preppy Pres — fell in love with an ordinary, chubby little sophomore named Kerry, who belonged to someone else.

CHAPTER

P res left the school immediately, heading for his red Porsche, breathing hard and telling himself not to be stupid. There is no such thing as instant love, he said to himself. Instant coffee, instant tea, but not instant love. And even if there is, I'm above stealing somebody else's girl. And even if I'm not above it, those were Andrew's eyes Kerry was looking into, not mine.

Pres didn't get as far as his Porsche.

Angie was sitting glumly on the wide steps.

"What are you doing here, Angie?" he asked irritably, taking it out on her. "It's freezing. There's probably ice on those steps. Get up." He took her elbow and helped her to her feet.

She said, "I forgot to ask anybody for a ride to Nancy's party, Pres, and I'm stranded, and anyway I don't want to go."

Pres sighed. Girls were always saying meaningless, contradictory things he could not interpret. This was a classic example. "Why don't you want to go?" he asked. "We won the game. And Nancy's parties are great. As for the ride, relax. I'll take you."

"I wasn't begging," said Angie.

"I know you weren't." Pres softened. Angie was irresistibly lovable. Even he, Pres, adored her, in a brotherly sort of way. Angie had been dating a college boy named Marc Filanno since spring, and the bond between Angie and Marc was as close as marriage, although he had a feeling probably not sexually that close. Angie was a very straight-laced girl with a stern upbringing.

Angie leaned against him in a tired sort of way, not a loving way. He felt her shiver through her heavy ski jacket. "Come on," he said, "let's get the heater going in my car."

They walked toward the Porsche, which was a hike away. Pres always parked as far away from other cars as he could, to prevent anybody from opening a door against his Porsche and maybe denting it.

"Oh, Pres! I miss him so much!" Angie said explosively. "Why did he have to go back to college? I feel amputated."

Normally Pres would have dismissed this remark as so much sentimental blather, but tonight he felt touched. The idea of being loved that much made him envy Marc fiercely. "He had to go back to college," said Pres reasonably. "How's he going to earn a living if he doesn't get his engineering degree? Give the guy a break, Angie."

"It's just that I hate going places by myself," said Angie.

"So come with me. I see myself in the role of chaperone. I think I've got real potential as a safe escort."

Angie and Pres laughed together. Pres's reputation was hardly that of a safe escort. Nobody who went back and forth between the likes of Vanessa and Mary Ellen could be considered a brotherly sort.

Squeezing his hand through her thick mitten, Angie said, "Thanks, Pres. I'm going to take you up on that. It's not that I feel Marc abandoned me, or doesn't love me. I'm just so lonely without him."

Even her voice grew thin, and he could feel the loneliness through the syllables that hung in the frosty night air. Pres ached.

Kerry, he thought. He tried to imagine Kerry feeling so lonely without him, and he smiled a little. Kerry didn't know he was alive. Kerry's eyes focused exclusively on Andrew.

Pres jumped when Andrew's voice rang across the nearly empty parking lot. "Angie!" shouted her younger brother. "Did you remember to arrange a ride home for Kerry and me, too?"

The Porsche was not designed for the comfort of four people, but Pres immediately turned and yelled, "Yes, she did. You're coming with us. Hurry up." He watched them hurry, Kerry nothing but a bundle of silvery grey in the thickness of her winter coat. As they passed under the lamplight, Kerry's cheeks stood out red and rounded and her hair peeked from under the hood that protected her ears. Pres gripped Angie a little tighter and Angie said, "I'm not slipping on the ice, Pres. Thanks anyway."

He relaxed. Andrew and Kerry caught up to them, laughing. Laughing together, Pres thought, wanting that shared laughter for himself. The two sophomores squeezed into the back of the Porsche and he envied Andrew, crushed against Kerry like that. "Why don't you two come to Nancy's party?" he said to them. He put the heater on high for Angie and directed the vents at her feet.

"Oh, we couldn't do that," said Kerry. "We weren't invited."

"Andrew's on the basketball team," Pres pointed out, "and I'm a cohost tonight because I'm supplying all the soda."

"Oh, that's wonderful," said Angie, turning in the seat to beam at her brother. "Yes. Pres is right. Come."

Angie's family had a closeness that Pres had often envied. Angie loved to have Andrew around. There had been a time when Pres and his parents were indivisible, too. When he was a kid — probably up through the sixth grade — he and his father had been inseparable, always fishing, watching football games on TV, going to look at the new car models, doing everything together. But the family had come apart in his adolescence. He did not know if it was his own fault or theirs.

It was the first time he had acknowledged,

even peripherally, that he might possibly have some responsibility in the disintegration of the Tilford family. He shrugged off the thought. At this point he did not care about his family. He cared about being near Kerry Elliot.

Kerry was bouncing happily on the seat. He watched her in the rear view mirror to the point that it endangered his driving. "Oh, Pres, thank you!" she cried. He realized that for Kerry this was pure excitement and honor: driving with a prestigious senior, sitting in his superlative car, setting off for the party of the month.

His eyes went briefly to Andrew. Andrew was like his sister Angie: not particularly good-looking, and yet so wholesome, so appealing, such a niceness to his demeanor that it was impossible not to like him. Even Pres, who felt affection for few and contempt for many, liked Andrew Poletti.

Great, Pres thought dismally. Five minutes have gone by and I'm already into a triangle with those two.

He parked near Nancy's covered pool, now a huge rectangle of old snow, and held the door open for Andrew and Kerry to get out. When Kerry awkwardly squeezed forward he caught her arm and helped her. She smiled up at him in thanks and his heart flipped.

Pres was utterly disgusted with himself. He was above this sort of thing. To get his mind off it and to keep himself from ripping Kerry away from Andrew and driving to California with her, he took Angie's arm instead.

Angie said, "Pres, darling, you're such a sweetheart."

Only Angie could possibly describe Pres as a sweetheart. Pres had traveled on the cliff between being mischievous and being dangerous for some time. He walked Angie to Nancy's house and they greeted Mrs. Goldstein.

He had not let go of Angie's arm because it was a way of keeping his thoughts in control — the dangerous disturbing thoughts he was entertaining about Kerry. He made himself look at Angie, but his thoughts continued to focus on Kerry. The thoughts turned to fantasies, and he thought he might just have to go take a swim in the lake to cool off.

Angie did not appear to notice Pres's attitude. Since meeting Marc, Angie had not considered another male human being, Pres thought. She'd never see Pres's starry eyes. If she did, she'd figure he was high on something and she'd insist on driving back, that was all.

Not that anybody at a party of Mrs. Goldstein's ever had an opportunity to get high on anything.

Finally he released Angie in order to go back to his car and get the soda, which he'd forgotten and which everyone was clamoring for, calling him various names for having left them thirsty for so long. He endured the teasing by the basketball jocks for his being a cheerleader, and gave it back to them as good as they gave him about the stupid moves they'd made during the game tonight.

Across the enormous room stood Vanessa Barlow.

Pres stiffened.

He could not immediately tell who she'd come with. She was standing in her own classic pose: hair swirled, legs apart, hands on hips. A tantalizing pose that half threatened, half beckoned. For once it did nothing to him.

There's something good in having a crush on Kerry after all, he thought, and the word caught at Pres. *Crush.* Stupid word. Only girls had crushes. Imagine *him*, Pres, having a crush.

He looked for Kerry. She was standing with Andrew and Angie by the fireplace, warming herself. The fire was roaring and her legs were outlined against flickering yellow tongues of fire. She'd taken off her ski jacket. She was wearing a very ordinary green pullover sweater and jeans. Her hair needed to be brushed or something — it was flyaway, nothing but disorder. He thought she was beautiful.

"Pres," said Troy, laughing, and punching him lightly. "What's the matter? You flipped out over Angie? Better watch yourself. Marc will put your lips back over your shoulder blades if you try kissing Angie."

Pres flushed. He could not remember such a thing happening to him before: actually going red over a girl. The two basketball players who witnessed this shouted with laughter and lowered their voices to say more to him that Mrs. Goldstein wouldn't overhear.

It was better that they should think it was

Angie than Kerry, Pres thought. He yanked himself free to go get the soda cases.

From her seat on the sofa, Mary Ellen Kirkwood watched him with fascination. *Pres* is interested in *Angie?* she thought. How amazing.

Pres had dated an awful lot of girls. His trick was to go out maybe two, three times at the most and just as the girl was getting sure that she had it made, he'd vanish. Only Mary Ellen and Vanessa had managed more than three dates with Pres.

But Angie?

Angie's mother, widowed years ago, had single-handedly raised her four children by running a beauty parlor in the basement of their split-level house. She worked very long and very hard and her standards were extremely high. Nothing Mary Ellen had ever seen made her believe those four children would consider doing anything that would upset their mother's standards. Angie was Marc's, Marc was Angie's — they might as well have taken vows on the subject.

So what was this look Pres kept sending in Angie's direction? Sure looked like love.

Mary Ellen stole a look at Vanessa. Vanessa was good at many things, but hiding her feelings was not one of them. Now a barely disguised rage disfigured her face.

Good, Mary Ellen thought. If *I* can't have Pres, I certainly don't want Vanessa to have him.

But she didn't want Angie to have problems either, and Pres, by and large, equaled problems.

29

I hope Angie can extricate herself from this easily, Mary Ellen thought. But she decided not to worry. Angie did not look as if she was any more aware of Pres than she was of Mr. Goldstein or the fireplace.

Mary Ellen tried the sour cream dip.

Of them all, only Walt Manners stood entirely on the sidelines. He was used to it. His popularity, which was enormous, never became intimate. He often thought it was because he had been brought up in his parents' profession.

The Manners Show.

His parents did a one-hour television show on the local station, five days a week. They spent their waking hours being peripherally involved in other people's joys, tragedies, occupations, successes, and needs.

All these kids passed before his eyes, and he spoke with them, laughed with them, and for the fourth year was cheering with them. He had virtually invented cheering for boys at Tarenton High. And yet he was not really a part of the gang. He might have been filming them, like his parents' crew — observing, doing a commentary.

He watched the various couples in the group come together, drift apart, and unite with other groups. Two girls here, two boys there, a boy and girl over on that side, a threesome behind him. Walt's own crush on Mary Ellen had tapered off, although he still liked her immensely. She reminded him of his mother: that same drive. She had made her choices in life and she would get there come hell or high water. Walt respected that. Much as he loved the sweet ones like Angie, Walt's heart was with the tough ones like Mary Ellen.

Observing Pres Tilford, Walt frowned slightly. What was this expression on Pres's face? If he didn't know better, Walt would say it was adoration. Pres, to whom the most important thing of all was to keep a distance from love? Pres, who had formed a friendship with Troy, surely the most distant person Walt had ever run into? Walt tried to figure out who was the object of this adoration, but failed.

Mary Ellen had three potato chips and stopped. Her self-control was relentless. Troy sat down next to her, self-control the last thing on his mind, and began alternately eating chips loaded with dip and kissing her cheek. Mary Ellen was startled. It was the first time he had ever done anything like that and she couldn't figure out what he was feeling. But then she rarely knew what he was feeling; he wanted it that way. It made him feel safer and it made her angry some of the time. But he was Troy Frederick and that meant something to her.

"I love those earrings," he said, touching them gently. "You look terrific, Mary Ellen."

To Mary Ellen, Troy was gentlemanly. She did not know if this attribute came from Eastern boarding schools or from his upbringing, but she had not run into it with any other boy. Even Walt, who was unfailingly pleasant and thoughtful, was not quite like this. The trouble was, she thought, unsure of her analysis, that good manners and a suave smile seemed to be all there was to Troy. Pres was a pain. A spoiled brat, moody, volatile — yet he had more substance. He was more interesting.

And of course Patrick. . . .

She sighed. When would the day come that she could wipe Patrick out of her mind? Patrick had more character than the five hundred boys at Tarenton High combined. Mary Ellen resented a fate that so twisted the things she yearned for.

At least Patrick was not at the party. Nancy sometimes invited him. All the girls adored Patrick. But without Patrick around, Mary Ellen could concentrate on Troy. Maybe find that scrap of personality she wanted in him.

Angie joined them. "Guess what!" she said, almost gurgling with delight.

"What?" Troy asked, smiling. Troy would always be the one who gave the right answers at the right cue lines; Troy would never leave you conversationally stranded, never leave you feeling awkward or embarrassed.

"I," said Angie importantly, "I, Angie Poletti, yes, *I* —"

Everyone began laughing. "We get the point, Angie. You, Angie Poletti, yes, you, have done something extraordinary."

Angie gave a little shiver of pleasure and hugged herself.

I bet she's engaged to Marc, Mary Ellen thought suddenly. Oh, Lord, don't let her drop out of school and marry him. Don't let Marc drop out of school, either!

Mary Ellen had very firm plans for the future: She was going to leave Tarenton a star, go to New York and become a bigger star in modeling and return occasionally for a day in Tarenton, perhaps to be interviewed by Walt's parents. Mary Ellen found people whose plans were non-existent or vague to be very annoying. It was *your* life out there! How could you just stroll into it, letting the events occur as they might? Mary Ellen had her future planned, and she intended no interference with it at all.

Knowing Angie, Angie was blithely assuming the future would be as good as the present, and she was simply drifting along.

"I," repeated Angie, beaming irresistibly at them all, *"I made honor roll!"*

It was the last thing they had expected her to say.

"You?" said Pres, speaking for them all. "Angie, you just barely scraped by last year! I remember you had to be tutored every afternoon after practice so you wouldn't flunk algebra."

"I know," said Angie. "But I think I've matured. My grey matter must be greyer this year. I finishing this marking period with three B's and an A."

They were cheerleaders, and this definitely called for a cheer.

Nancy, because it was her house and she could take the risk, leaped up on the long, sturdy table in the middle of the room, did a pirouette, and yelled, "Let's have a cheer for Angie!"

Immediately the squad burst into an assortment of herky jumps, banana jumps, splits, whoops, and hollers. The basketball team and their dates looked slightly bemused, but joined in the general celebration. They hadn't heard the reason for the cheering and of course assumed they were the only ones worth cheering for.

Nancy leaped gracefully down from the table, ignoring her mother's faintly annoyed look and her boyfriend Alex's delight. Alex Hague was always willing to watch Nancy move. Nancy hugged Angie. "Congratulations," she said. "I'm really proud of you."

Although the truth was that Nancy was really not thinking of the word "proud." She was actually amazed. Angie was not smart. Angie was average. She would not go on to college because she was neither academic nor shrewd. Honor roll? thought Nancy, who had to work to stay there herself. How astonishing.

What were the rest thinking? Nancy checked expressions.

But she immediately forgot that. Vanessa Barlow was standing there. Vanessa had crashed the party. Why, you hateful person! Nancy thought. I'd *never* ask you to my party. Not after the rotten things you've done. Just recently she had tried to get Mary Ellen and Nancy kicked off the squad. She had let Nancy's parents know Nancy was dating Alex, knowing they wouldn't approve of him, and that Nancy had made sure they wouldn't meet.

34

Alex was different from anybody Nancy, or her parents, knew. He was a musician, a New Wave kind of boy, whose hair was dyed blond, and who wore bizarre clothes and an earring in one ear. He appeared to be dangerous and funky, but in reality he was kind and funny and dear. Once her parents met him, however, once they heard him play the piano — Mozart at that — they realized he was a decent, nice guy.

Nancy could ask her mother to do something about Vanessa. But what? They could hardly lift Vanessa bodily and throw her into the lake, appealing though the idea was.

How nice it would be if Vanessa were to elope with a kid from Florida and never be seen in the north country again. But probably kids from Florida were too smart to fall into Vanessa's hands.

Nancy sighed. She would just enjoy Alex, who was *always* a pleasure, and thereby manage to avoid kicking a guest, although an uninvited guest, in the shins. But as always, Alex had vanished on her. He had an uncanny ability to slip away. How someone as handsome as Alex could be unnoticeable, Nancy could not imagine. But it happened time after time.

She went in search of him. He was in the front hall, helping Pres carry soda in. He was closing the door with his foot, arms full of soda cans. Nancy laughed and tickled Alex lightly. "You want me to drop these cans?" he responded.

"Yes. For me, you should drop everything."

Alex grinned and let go of 48 cans. Nancy shrieked, leaping back to save her toes. "I take you seriously," Alex told her.

Pres said, "You guys get to drink from the dented ones."

Nancy looked down. They weren't just dented. Two of them had opened and were oozing ginger ale all over the floor.

"Forget it," Alex said. "It's not a carpet, it's slate. We can clean it up when we get around to it."

"I think that should be now," Nancy said.

"Nah. *This* should be now." Stepping over the chaos of cans, Alex took Nancy in his arms. Nancy kissed him, thinking, I am so lucky to have Alex! She felt ginger ale soak through her socks and dampen her toes. She wouldn't have traded the moment for anything.

In Nancy's living room, where mouths were dry and salty from too many chips and no soda, four girls stood gossiping. One of them whispered, "I have heard something really awful."

The rest, attracted by such a low voice, said, "What?"

"Well, don't tell anybody because it's just a rumor, but I heard that Mary Ellen got that fabulous outfit she's wearing by shoplifting it from Marnie's."

They all gasped. Involuntarily their eyes flew to Mary Ellen. She looked wonderful, but Mary Ellen would look terrific in cast-offs. Nobody had expected her to be in such a glamorous outfit. She'd worn it to school and been overdressed, she was so proud of it. Tonight, by firelight, it was perfect.

And how well Troy complemented her. Troy rarely wore casual clothes; he was one of the few boys in school given to appearing in a sports jacket and tie. Mary Ellen was basking in Troy's admiration. The girls were faintly jealous. Imagine moving effortlessly from Patrick to Pres to Walt (whom she ignored) to Troy.

"Are you kidding about that shoplifting stuff?" Shelley Eismar said.

"No, she's not," put in Vanessa. "I heard it myself. And you have to admit, it is amazing she's wearing something from Marnie's. Mary Ellen is the poorest of the poor."

They regarded Mary Ellen. Cathleen Eismar, Shelley's twin, said, "Maybe she got a big birthday check and blew it on that."

Nobody believed that for a moment.

"Although," Vanessa said thoughtfully, "I have heard that the department store at the mall has had a terrible time lately with shoplifting. Their store managers were in talking to Mrs. Oetjen just last week."

Mrs. Oetjen was their principal. A warm, motherly woman, she was, however, inflexible when it came to punishment. No charming smile, no quivering lip, no clever excuse ever got any Tarenton kid out of a serious situation. You did something wrong — well, you found out the consequences in a hurry.

"All that doesn't mean a thing," said Susan Yardley stoutly. "Mary Ellen could have a job and be earning money."

"Forget that," said Cathleen. "This is the beginning of basketball season. When Mary Ellen doesn't have a game, she's got practice."

"Besides," Vanessa pointed out, "she'd be kicked off Varsity if she was working fifteen or twenty hours a week. She couldn't do that and get good grades and still manage cheerleading."

"I think," Shelley Eismar said, "that I'll just ask Mary Ellen how she managed to pay for that."

Vanessa egged her on. Shelley probably would have done it, too, except that Vanessa's cruelty had hurt her once or twice and she was slowed by a sense of charity.

Troy and Mary Ellen began dancing, a mesmerizing, intimate dance that made everybody else want to imitate them. Very close, very slow. The kids who had come as couples followed suit. Those who were alone stationed themselves busily by the food or each other, trying to look as though they didn't care in the least that they weren't in somebody's arms, eyes closed, body shifting sensuously to slow music.

The music turned to pulsing rock.

A steady, hypnotic beat filled the room.

And the rumor about Mary Ellen moved like the dancers — slowly, tantalizingly, entwining the room, until it had circled Mary Ellen like a poisonous vine.

CHAPTER

Troy took Mary Ellen home.

At first she had refused to allow boys to come to her house. She would meet them somewhere instead and get picked up by her parents. But it was too cumbersome to continue. Eventually she had to give in to the inevitable: Any boy who dated her arrived on the quiet, shabby street where her house sat identical to all the other aluminum-sided tract houses. Identical except for its color: a particularly loud shade of turquoise that in Mary Ellen's mind screamed *poor, tasteless, lower class* at the top of its lungs.

She hated her house.

It was difficult to imagine hating a mere building the way she hated that house. It was a bottled hate, because she loved her parents and could not hold them responsible for not providing the kind of life she would have liked to have. They did the best they could.

Troy.

Rich, casual, sophisticated Troy lived like Pres in a dozen large, impressive rooms filled with lovely, expensive things. He had no idea what it was to share a tiny bedroom with a younger, messier sister. To share a single closet with her, too, so that all your clothing was always wrinkled and had to be ironed every morning.

Oh, to be rich! Mary Ellen thought. She touched the earrings again, her first really good pieces of jewelry. This is what I'm going to have, she thought. No matter what I have to do to get them, this is the beginning of how I'm going to live — surrounded by pretty things.

Tomorrow I'll go to Marnie's again, she decided.

Troy stopped his car in her driveway. He touched her lightly and she needed no urging, but slid across to touch him, and snuggling against him, she kissed him first. Their thick winter clothing was a stimulant rather than a hindrance, because it made things so secret and so hidden. They began kissing each other's throats and Troy's lips moved to her ears and she wondered what it was like to kiss an earring and she laughed slightly, kissing his hair and forehead and finally his lips.

She was not really kissing Troy Frederick, but what he symbolized — wealth, position, manners. She tried hard to make him think she was wildly attracted to him, but she wasn't sure she was succeeding.

They might have gone on for some time except that Mary Ellen began to yawn. Troy pulled away. "That's the second time you've done that to me, Mary Ellen," he said stiffly. "Making out is such a bore, isn't it? A girl can hardly stay awake."

She forced an embarrassed laugh. "I stay up so late studying, Troy. And it was a long night. Long game, long party, and I have to get up early tomorrow."

"Tomorrow's Saturday," Troy protested. "You can sleep in."

Mary Ellen was evasive. But she had chosen the right boy to be evasive with; Troy so intensely disliked being pressed for details of his own life that he would never demand to know why she had to get up early. Either she volunteered the information or it wasn't his business.

He asked her out for Saturday and she said, "All right," but with a slight hesitation.

Troy had not expected her to hesitate. Had she been hoping for a better offer from someone else? Or did she have to rearrange her schedule to go out Saturday? Or perhaps she wasn't sure she really wanted to go out with him again.

He did not like to contemplate what existed between two people. Better never to think of relationships at all than to let them tangle you up. If Mary Ellen came, then they would have a good time; and if she didn't, then he would do something else, that's all.

He kissed her again in a rather businesslike way, almost as if he was kissing her because he felt he should. She told him what a fine basketball player he was and how she loved cheering for him, and she ran into her house.

Mary Ellen knew that Troy dated her for the same reasons that Pres used to date her — because she was beautiful, a cheerleader, and it added to his image to have her with him. But his reason for taking her out didn't bother Mary Ellen . . . she was getting what she wanted, too — dates with a rich, socially acceptable boy. When it came to anything else, anything physical, the only boy who interested Mary Ellen was Patrick. There was hardly a day that she didn't think about the excitement of kissing him, of the tender way he held her, and of the unquestioning love he had for her. But Patrick was not what Mary Ellen had in mind for a boyfriend.

It wasn't really very late. Mary Ellen had wanted to go home when the party was still going strong. Troy didn't want to go to his house. He was still flying high from winning the game, from making his share of saves and baskets. He knew he wouldn't go to sleep until two in the morning and he didn't have to get up early; there was no one who cared what he did on Saturday. Troy drove aimlessly, trying to decide whether to go back to Nancy's party or do something else. When he passed the Hamburg King, there was a band of high school kids and he stopped and went in.

They waved and moved slightly to indicate seating space and a welcome. He went to the counter, got a large fries and a milkshake, and joined a bunch of boys. There was safety in boys — none of the undercurrent of indefinable feelings or confusion that reigned when the girls were there, too.

"Well, I think it's too bad," one of the boys said. "I mean, it's such a wholesome-looking group. You'd think you could tell. But no. They turn out to be as rotten as anybody else. I really feel lousy about the whole thing."

"What whole thing?" Troy said.

"Shoplifting. It's such a grubby little crime. And I hate to think of Mary Ellen Kirkwood as grubby."

Troy stared at him.

"But the worst is Angie," put in another boy. "She's supposed to be such an angel. She even looks like one. Like her mother knew Angela was the right name at birth. Tonight it's all over town she cheated her way onto the honor roll."

Troy was as stunned as if they'd bludgeoned him. He knew Angie only slightly but his immediate judgment of her was that she *was* angelic. Cheating? Angie? And what on earth could they mean about Mary Ellen? *Grubby?*

"Angie's not exactly a brain," said another boy. "My girl friend told me she's had tutors for two years running to get good enough grades to stay on Varsity Cheerleading, and here she is on the honor roll."

"It's the whole squad," the first boy said. "I mean, this is supposed to be Tarenton's finest, right? And what do we hear from the kids at Garrison? That it's Tarenton's *worst.*"

"I can't get over Mary Ellen shoplifting,

43

though," the second boy said. "Everybody's talking about it. New clothes, new jewelry, new shoes. Right out of nowhere, no explanations, no cash. I guess if you get desperate enough, you'll do anything."

"I always heard shoplifting was kind of a sport with girls, though," objected one of them. "Not because they need to."

"Mary Ellen's got a sport," the first said. "Boys. She's stealing stuff because she can't get it any other way."

Troy could not speak to defend her. He had just held her in his arms, touched his lips to hers — and here he was silent when she needed support. I'm a crud, he thought. I've got to tell them she'd never do that. I've got to tell them to shut up.

But he hated to speak up. He felt no loyalty to Mary Ellen, and he wasn't interested in putting his own hide on the line.

"How can you be sure?" Troy asked.

"It's all over town, Troy. Mary Ellen lusts for things and if she has to steal to get them, she will."

Just be careful with Mary Ellen, Pres had said to him. She's a great girl, but she's in this for what she can get. Prestige, money, cars, dates.

Troy could feel himself abandoning Mary Ellen the way he had abandoned so many other people . . . or been abandoned. Each of his parents had been through three spouses; each was off honeymooning with a fourth. He had enough stepparents and stepcousins and stepgrandparents

44

to start a new town. They came and went from his life, all with their own fairly pleasant way of dealing with disaster: rarely fighting, rarely yelling, just ending the marriage as if it were merely a season, like basketball or soccer.

Troy had never felt too damaged by this. He had remained separate from it, as much as possible. But he knew now how great the damage had been. A girl he liked, a girl he found impressive, needed support based on faith and he, Troy, was not going to give it.

He played with his French fries, which were cold, and finally tossed them in the garbage. He said good-bye and drove home alone, the thrill of beating Garrison entirely forgotten.

Angie telephoned Marc.

She loved hearing his voice. It was very deep. A robust baritone that filled her life as well as the telephone lines. She could not remember her life before Marc and had not once imagined a future without him.

They talked for an hour. Listening to his voice was like making love. Marc said pleadingly, "Can't you come up for a weekend, Angie?"

"You know I have a basketball game every Friday and Saturday for the next month, Marc. *You* come *here*."

Marc lowered his voice. "Look, Angie. I share an apartment with two other guys. Both of them are going to be away next weekend. You could come up. I know another girl coming up from Tarenton who could give you a ride. I'd pay the gasoline. This is a nice apartment. You'd like it. The two of us. No interruptions."

"I hear you," Angie said, "and I have a game."

"So get a substitute to cheer for you. Put me first for a change."

"Marc, I always put you first!" she protested.

He said that if she really put him first, she would understand what it was doing to him, going without her like this. He was going crazy.

"How crazy?" said Angie. "It isn't like we're sleeping together, Marc. I miss you, too, and I miss you enough that it hurts, but it isn't fair to lay some guilt on me. I'm a cheerleader, I have an obligation, and even if your roommates are away till next Fourth of July I'm not going to spend the night."

"How about if they're away till the fifth of July?" Marc said.

They both laughed. Angie changed the subject swiftly. "I made honor roll, Marc. *Me*. Isn't that exciting? All my studying is paying off."

"Go on. You never study. When you and I are together, all you do is kiss me. You learn every inch of my skin, not every word of your textbooks."

"It's more fun that way," Angie said.

"Don't!" pleaded Marc. "Come up this weekend. A happy couple is a couple that's done everything."

"Forget it, Great American Stud. Take six cold showers and an aspirin and see me in two weeks at my house."

"With your mother, your sister, and your two

46

brothers in attendance," Marc said. "Great."

"It *is* great," Angie said. "You're unbelievably lucky to be a part of my family."

Marc conceded that this was true. It was just that he wanted to be a more *intimate* part. Their talk went on and on, neither changing, neither wanting to hang up.

Olivia stood nude in front of her mirror, brushing her hair with a violence she would have preferred to apply to her mother. She was standing bare because it offended her mother. "Put on a robe," Mrs. Evans said twice. "Please put on a robe."

"I'm perfectly comfortable, Mother."

"You can't possibly be comfortable. You have your window open and there's an arctic wind going through here."

"I can't live in a greenhouse, Mother. I have to have air. Now what is your problem, Mother? Just *say* it. You're driving me crazy, dropping hints and innuendos."

Mrs. Evans alternately stared at and avoided her daughter's body. The scars from the repetitive surgery were such a contrast to the supple athlete's body. "Put on a flannel nightgown," she said crossly. "You know I was against this cheerleading from the very start."

Olivia brushed so hard she almost removed her scalp. She did not care what her mother's attitude was toward cheering. I *love* it, she thought. They can have their angelic Angies; their beautiful, popular Mary Ellens; and their rich, graceful Nancys. I, Olivia, am the real gymnast. I'm the one who does the flips and tumbles and the breathtaking falls from Pres's shoulders.

"I heard the most horrible things tonight," Mrs. Evans said. "I nearly died at the idea of my daughter being associated with this sort of thing, and I won't have it. I'm going to have conferences with Mrs. Engborg and Mrs. Oetjen on Monday."

The coach and the principal? "What are you talking about?" Olivia demanded.

"Mary Ellen Kirkwood is some kind of thief. Everyone was saying so. She's a shoplifter, although she hasn't been caught yet. The last few weeks she's been running around with enough new jewelry to decorate a Christmas tree. I won't have my daughter associating with that kind of trash."

Olivia hurled the hairbrush across the room. "I never heard such junk! Mary Ellen doesn't shoplift. She's honorable. I have a lot of respect for Mary Ellen. You just want me off the squad and you're grabbing at any excuse to accomplish it."

"That's not true! I think the squad is a danger to your health. That fall you did tonight, where Walt threw you in the air and Pres caught you and then you vaulted off his shoulders — you could break your neck doing that. But that isn't the point."

"Oh, no," said Olivia sarcastically. "Not much."

48

"The point is that my daughter must not be associated with girls who are running around shoplifting and cheating."

"Now you're accusing Mary Ellen of cheating as well?" said Olivia. "Mother, cut it out. Mary Ellen has been on the honor roll all her life and she'll go right on being on High Honors, and she doesn't need to cheat to do it. She —"

"Not Mary Ellen. It's Angie Poletti who's cheating. Even her last year's English teacher was remarking on it. He said it was absolutely amazing that Angie could get three B's and an A."

"Oh, Mother, I can't stand this. This is the kind of trashy thing you would say about my doctors, back when they wanted to do surgery you didn't want them to do. You'll say anything to get what you want. You want me off that squad and you're going to spread these ghastly rumors to do it. I think you should be ashamed of yourself."

Olivia literally escorted her mother to her bedroom door and slammed it behind her. "Goodnight!" she hollered. The door didn't slam hard enough to suit Olivia, so she opened it and slammed it again. This jarred the perfume bottles on her dresser hard enough that Olivia had to leap back and catch two of them before they hit the floor.

She juggled the tiny glass bottles lightly from hand to hand.

Rumors. What terrible rumors.

Olivia's mother rarely conversed with the other parents. Other parents were proud of their athletic children and took snapshots of them and hollered for them and threw parties for them. Only Mrs. Evans wanted her daughter to drop out and stay safely at home, having weak tea and toast. So if her mother had heard these rumors, then *everybody* was repeating them. Loudly enough that even Mrs. Evans could not miss them.

I went through so much to get on the squad! Olivia thought.

On the wall were the photographs of what she had been through. Thin and debilitated before her heart surgery. Afterwards, in gymnastics classes, dancing, fencing. And now the moment had arrived, the moment she had craved so much: Her body was obeying her every command, and she was a member of the Varsity Squad of Tarenton High School.

Rumors like this would tear the squad apart.

Tear apart all that Olivia was enjoying so much.

And if they were true. . . .

Olivia shuddered. They could not be true. She would not believe it of Mary Ellen Kirkwood or of Angie Poletti.

CHAPTER

Walt Manners loved driving home.

He had a Jeep, which was fun to drive because it was so tough, so high on the road. Their driveway was three fifths of a mile long, way out of Tarenton in the woods. Rutted and rocky, the drive wound through hemlocks and over narrow brooks and arrived in the clearing his father had carved with a chain saw years ago.

The Manners house was an interesting combination of log cabin and modern glass. Most of the filming of the television hour was done in their living room, the left half of which was the old original log cabin, and the right half of which was a glass wall looking out to the thick forest beyond.

It was very late. Nancy's party had not ended until one o'clock when her mother gently shooed everyone out. Walt was coming home by moonlight, and the house and clearing lay peacefully beneath the stars. The wind shivered softly through the bare branches, and when he cut the motor he could hear the trees scraping lightly.

He parked the Jeep in the barn and walked to the kitchen door. There were few lights on, so he expected his parents to be asleep, but they were waiting up for him. The Manners family had to talk so much at work that they tended toward silence among themselves. The greeting was silent: a hug from his mother and a wave from his father.

They were sipping coffee. At this hour, probably Sanka. Walt fixed himself a cup and sat with them. His parents liked Friday nights. No pressure of a show in the morning. Although they probably would tape segments in Garrison the next day, they could schedule this as they chose.

"Great game," Walt told his parents. "We thrashed Garrison good. And Nancy's party was terrific."

His parents smiled at him and nodded.

Walt often wondered how other families worked. Pres's, for example. He was willing to bet they talked a lot in that family, and most of it angry talk.

Angie's family. A nice one. Walt did not know of a family any closer. Angie always hugged her brothers hello and they always hugged her. Angie's boyfriends were virtually adopted into the family whether they liked it or not. Walt's impression was that they always liked it and grieved when it was over.

Mary Ellen? Hard to say. Walt barely knew

her parents: grey-looking people, who lit up like candles when they watched their beautiful, capable daughter. Their pride in Mary Ellen knew no bounds. And as for Mary Ellen's little sister, Gemma, she absolutely believed that Mary Ellen was perfect.

But Walt didn't envy anyone. He had a good life, good parents, a good home. Different, obviously. At all hours of the day and night they were invaded by an endless series of total strangers whose stories would be told in his living room.

He said, "So what are you planning for next week, Mom?"

"Well, we had an interesting request from the manager at the department store at Tarenton Mall," his mother said. "They've been having a bad time with teenage shoplifting. They're hoping if we do a segment, it will awaken parents to what their children are doing and lower the shoplifting rate. Have you heard anything at school about shoplifting, Walt? We don't want you to be a snitch or anything. I'm just curious to know if kids ever talk about it. Brag about doing it for fun or some such thing."

Walt shrugged. He was not someone who cared terribly about acquiring things. He rarely spent money and rarely thought about spending money. He enjoyed school, loved cheerleading, and loved all winter sports, from cross-country skiing to ice fishing. For Walt, the pleasure lay in doing, not buying. "I don't think they'd tell me if they did," he said. "But I'll keep my ears open."

His father said, "I thought we'd talk to your

principal, Mrs. Oetjen. She's a pretty interesting woman; that time we interviewed her about falling college board scores, she managed to make it fascinating. And we'll get in touch with the police and talk about arrest records. Then we'll want to interview kids who admit to shoplifting."

Walt was incredulous. "Nobody would admit it to you, Dad."

"Sure they would. People love to be on television. Promise them anonymity. Do a tape without cameras — just the voice."

"But Tarenton's a small town," Walt protested. "Somebody at the high school would be bound to recognize the voice." He felt sick at the thought.

His father simply continued his plans. "The department store has not had a policy of prosecuting. They felt it was bad publicity. But they've changed their minds. They're going to take every single person to court who shoplifts so much as a lipstick."

Well, nobody Walt knew *would* shoplift so much as a lipstick. Walt lost interest and ceased to listen to his parents. He yawned. The yawn made him think of Mary Ellen, who had spent half the evening trying to mask her yawns. He was not sure why she'd be so sleepy. She couldn't be keeping any schedule other than the one he was, and *he* wasn't tired.

Walt pictured Mary Ellen with Troy. A few months ago, it would have destroyed him because his crush on Mary Ellen had been so intense. Now he felt only an almost brotherly interest in her.

She was part of the squad, and cheerleading was crucial to Walt.

Waking instantly, Mary Ellen Kirkwood slammed her hand down on the alarm clock half-way through the first ring. She checked to be sure Gemma hadn't been disturbed. No. Her sister Gemma slept soundly, head under her pillow, thick quilts heaped over her indistinguishable little body.

Mary Ellen slid out of bed and shivered uncontrollably when her bare feet hit bare wood. She tiptoed into the bathroom and dressed in the clothes she'd laid out the night before. Five-thirty in the morning. What an ungodly hour. In the kitchen, she downed a small glass of orange juice, chewed on a tasteless bagel, and checked her purse to be sure the rolls of quarters were there. Then she began emptying the living room of laundry bags.

Four for Mrs. Holmes. Six for Mrs. Aiken. One for Mr. and Mrs. Cassio and one each for the three bachelors at number eleven.

She carried them out the door to her father's beat-up station wagon. She hoisted an enormous box of detergent, a huge bottle of Clorox, some fabric softener, and her book bag into the front seat and set out for the laundromat.

She began yawning uncontrollably.

How long can I keep this up? Mary Ellen thought, shivering at the same time. The wagon's heater wasn't yet warmed up enough to unfreeze her blood. I've been doing laundry for four weeks now and I'm already a basket case. I can't even stay awake for Troy! What do I do if this yawning hits me during a basketball game some night?

Rah-rah (yawn) Taren (yawn) *ton.*
Go, Big (yawn) Red, *Go.*

She hated doing other people's laundry, but she couldn't get a job through the high school placement office. If she were to apply, her coach would state that she couldn't work *and* be a cheerleader, and the counselor would send someone else to be interviewed.

That left babysitting, which paid nothing. So she was doing laundry for the working people on her block instead. She had so many customers that it was clear Mary Ellen was meeting an important need. She tried to feel virtuous. But she didn't feel virtuous. She felt exhausted.

Mary Ellen sorted laundry, took notes to remember whose was in what machine, added detergent, set water temperatures, and dropped in quarters. So many quarters. A lifetime of quarters.

By six-ten she had all the loads going.

She opened her bookbag, took out her history book, and began working on chapter nineteen. European history. She could not get interested in it. She did not know when she had run into a harder subject. Who could care about treaties, wars, kings, territories, religious splits, and more wars? Mary Ellen did not want to know the significance of Bismarck, the Treaty of Westphalia, or the Austro-Prussian War. But she did want an A.

A major exam was coming up. All those dates to memorize! 1066. 1588. Who cared? The only date in all history Mary Ellen was absolutely sure of was her own birthdate.

She fantasized about becoming so famous that one day all high school students would be forced to memorize the birthdate of Mary Ellen Kirkwood. She had not yet begun studying when the first machine stopped. Now drying, folding, packing up, Mary Ellen thought first of the three boys in her life: Patrick, for whom she yearned, body and soul; Troy, who was dating her; and Pres, who wasn't much interested anymore. Her mind wandered to Angie, and she wondered how she could have made honor roll last marking period — and have every expectation of making it again this marking period.

She went back to the three boys, especially to Patrick. If only you could choose a crush ahead of time, like a dress for a dance. But crushes came upon you, like a disease, and you were stuck. Like being stuck with your family and your family's income.

And your neighbors' laundry, she thought.

She folded undershirts for Mr. Cassio. She folded bedsheets for Mrs. Aiken, whose son was clearly not making it through the night without wetting the bed. She tried to remember who had been king, chancellor, prime minister, ambassador to or president of all those countries in all those generations of European history. Mary

Ellen groaned. "The only time I want to see Germany," she said to the empty laundromat, "is when I'm modeling there and they've photographed me against a backdrop of a castle in the Black Forest. As for England, I'm willing to marry Prince Andrew but otherwise I pass on learning facts about that country."

Pass.

She not only had to pass, she had to get A's, because she had to prove that a girl could be beautiful and a cheerleader and smart, too.

Mary Ellen finished the laundry as the laundromat began to fill up with all the tired, hardworking people whose Saturday mornings were devoted year round to laundry, groceries, and errands.

By eleven she had delivered her loads, received her pay, and gotten home. She added her Saturday laundry income to her Monday and Tuesday night income. Those nights she was at the laundromat from about ten until one in the morning. Her parents didn't mind. The laundromat was down the street from the firehouse and next door to a motel; it was safe at any hour. Mary Ellen counted up her money.

Earning money never failed to excite her. Sometimes she thought money was even more thrilling than boys. Today she had enough to buy that necklace in Marnie's, the one that matched her earrings. Real gold. A thin serpentine strand, as golden as Mary Ellen herself, and on it was a trio of fragile hearts.

Almost trembling with desire for the necklace,

Mary Ellen caught the bus (her mother had taken the station wagon to do errands) and took it to the shopping mall. She found Marnie's irresistible and went there constantly to gaze. This would be only the fourth time she had been able to buy anything there.

The sales clerk lowered her new necklace gently into a bed of cotton, closed the lid of the box, and put Mary Ellen's purchase into the beautiful, flowered bag that was Marnie's hallmark. It seemed too unsophisticated to let the clerk in Marnie's know how eager she was to wear it, so Mary Ellen carried her bag into the ladies' room to put it on. She had worn just the right outfit for it: her best sweater, with a dipping neckline to show off the necklace and her throat to best advantage.

Being poor makes you so much more eager, she thought, admiring the image in the mirror. You don't just want things a little bit. You ache and burn for them.

She went out into the department store to look at clothes for juniors. It would be another few weeks before she could afford anything more, but she would know long in advance exactly what she wanted. Maybe put it on layaway.

The Eismar twins and Vanessa Barlow were there, trying on clothes. Shelley and Cathleen Eismar had tried out for Varsity Cheerleading, but ended up on the Pompon Squad. Shelley and Cathy were nice girls, but they hadn't gotten over their disappointment at failing to make Varsity. Vanessa, however, was thoroughly rotten. There was no way you could ever pretend she was nice. Vanessa wasn't just disappointed, she was downright bitter. She had refused to go on Pompon Squad, which she said was for rejects. Vanessa wanted the top or nothing. Varsity or nothing. Pres Tilford or nothing.

Shelley, Cathy, and Vanessa were hardly Mary Ellen's favorite trio. But she had known them all her life and she could hardly pretend they weren't there. "Hi," she said cheerfully, walking over to see what they were buying. Knowing the Barlow and Eismar families, the girls were getting anything they wanted, and charging it, too.

"Love that necklace," said Shelley instantly. "Where'd you get it?"

"Here, at Marnie's," Mary Ellen said, basking in the whole idea of being able to shop there at last. For the first time in her life, she was dressed as well as anybody else, from her shoes to her necklace, from the scent of her perfume to her new lacy underpants.

The twins and Vanessa exchanged funny looks. Mary Ellen was jarred. She didn't like that look. It was sly . . . said something she didn't know . . . left her out.

"You working these days?" Vanessa asked.

Instantly Mary Ellen was afraid. Had they seen her? Did they know? Vanessa would report Mary Ellen in a heartbeat. Ardith Engborg would not give Mary Ellen a second chance, either. There would be another tryout to fill Mary Ellen's slot, and these three girls would be among the handful called up to try out for it.

Mary Ellen felt cold. "No," she said. "Whatever gave you that idea? How could I possibly have time to work, what with basketball season and homework and all?"

Vanessa nodded thoughtfully, as if this were a particularly interesting conclusion she wouldn't have drawn herself. Then she and the twins walked away. They didn't say good-bye. They didn't talk about the clothes draped over their arms. They just went.

What is this all about? Mary Ellen thought, staring at them. I know they were upset at tryouts, but that was ages ago. Surely they've gotten over it by now.

The girls stopped over at the register to charge their purchases. Their eyes flickered back to Mary Ellen, and there was something dark and scornful in those glances that made Mary Ellen quiver the way she had not done since second grade, when she didn't know anybody the first day of school and the teacher was mean.

Mary Ellen left the store quickly. Moments later she leaped back into its sheltering overhang just as Patrick Henley's garbage truck swooshed through a puddle in the parking lot. She didn't jump to avoid the water nearly as much as to avoid Patrick.

Why did she still come unglued over Patrick?

She literally had her pick of boys. How many girls could say that? If she got tired of Troy, why then she could move on to Walt.

But no, she had to ache for Patrick. She never

saw him, never visualized him, without yearning for him.

Patrick stopped the truck when he saw Mary Ellen and walked over to her. She backed away when she looked at his coveralls. They were clean, for some reason Patrick always looked clean, but still they were coveralls. Patrick grinned when he saw her move away from him. He knew her so well, every feeling she had, especially what she felt and didn't feel for him. He knew that just as he couldn't be near her without wanting her, she felt that way about him.

To tease her, to irritate her, to let her know, in his macho way, that he was stronger than she was, he grabbed her and kissed her. She started to fight him off and then just let her feelings take over. She didn't care who was watching; she kissed him back as wildly as he was kissing her.

Then she pushed him with as much strength as she had, and he stumbled backward. He grinned, waved at her, and went back to the truck.

Mary Ellen shook herself, as if she could shake off the feelings she had for Patrick. She didn't want them for Patrick anyhow. She wanted those feelings to sweep over her when she saw Pres Tilford, and she wanted Pres Tilford swept just as hard, and she wanted Pres and Mary Ellen to cheer together and love together.

And I've got Troy, she thought ruefully. Troy, who was cool and hard to understand.

Her long, red fingernails caressed the lovely necklace. At least *some* things in life worked out perfectly.

CHAPTER

The squad was working on a new cheer that Olivia had designed. It was a pyramid with Olivia on top. The final words were:

> If you tangle with us —
> You . . . *fall!*

at which point the pyramid collapsed in a heap. It was a funny cheer, a variety hard to come by, and although it was difficult to do because it was so easy to hurt each other, they wanted it for Wednesday night. They were going against Wickfield, whose Warriors were third-ranked and whom they had to beat in order to stay number one in the league.

The bottom row consisted of Walt, Pres, and Angie. Because of symmetry, Angie had to be in the middle, thus taking more of the weight load than either of the boys. By the seventh time they had rehearsed the fall, Angie could not take it any longer.

"All right," Ardith Engborg said, "let's break." She paused, and then smiled. They didn't see her smile that often and it was a relief to six kids used to a frown and a demand to try it again.

"In fact," she said, "let's quit for the day. You've worked very hard and obviously nobody had a restful weekend. Mary Ellen, I believe you have yawned ten times in as many minutes. Now you go home and take a nap, you hear?"

Mary Ellen nodded.

But the person who really heard Mrs. Engborg was Troy. He was sitting with Andrew and Kerry on the bleachers, watching the practice while he did his trigonometry. Mary Ellen wouldn't study with me Monday night, Troy thought. She said she studied better alone. And she said she can't study with me tonight, either. And of course tomorrow, Wednesday, is the big game so she won't be studying at all then.

What's she doing on Monday and Tuesday nights?

I don't believe she's studying alone.

Troy was deeply ashamed of his failure to defend Mary Ellen in front of the other boys. He wanted to be seen in public with her, to stand as a silent testimony of his support, but if she was out with some other guy, perhaps she neither needed nor wanted his support.

Pres had told him some of her background. Patrick adored her. Walt was just getting over a crush on her. But Walt never looked at Mary

Ellen like that anymore, and Patrick was never around.

So she studies alone, Troy told himself. So big deal. Don't get uptight about it. It doesn't ever pay to get uptight about other people. Especially girls.

Pres said in a loud voice, "Listen everybody. Want to come over to my house? Nobody can say he's got something else to do because we had another hour of practice scheduled." Pres faced the risers and yelled at Troy, Kerry, and Andrew. "Come on! My house!"

They were amazed and delighted. Pres inviting people over? Privately Mary Ellen figured Pres had had a fight with his parents the night before and was doing this to upset them, but still, she wanted very much to go. Even when they'd dated, Mary Ellen rarely got to Pres's house. His parents were not particularly welcoming to Pres's friends.

"I'll drive you, Angie," said Pres. "Don't worry about a ride."

Angie gave him a hug in response. Angie's hugs were given to everybody in the entire high school without discrimination, so this meant nothing to anybody. Pres called over his shoulder to Angie's brother Andrew. "Come on, with us, Andrew. You and Kerry can —"

"No, thanks, Pres," Andrew yelled back. "Walt said he'd take us, and his car is a little roomier for passengers anyhow."

There was nothing Pres could do but smile and agree. So how do I get Kerry alone? he thought.

Then he thought, What a stupid thing to wonder about. Even if I *do* get Kerry alone, what comes next? I fall on my knees? Beg her to give up Andrew for me? Sure. Believe it.

Arm around Angie, he led the way out of the gym. None of them changed from practice clothes this time. They were much too glad to be able to escape early from Ardith's demands, and they weren't going to give her time to reconsider. Or give Pres time either, for that matter. Most of them had never been to Pres's house.

Normally cheerleading practice ended quite a bit later, when the school was utterly deserted. But today the late bus had not even left yet. The foyer was still filled with kids in various postures of boredom, waiting for the bus or their rides. The cheerleaders threaded their way through the foyer, greeting friends, knowing themselves marked out by their unity. Every one of the six loved the fact of being Varsity together, on display.

Mary Ellen could not help the feeling of triumph that always came over her when she saw the various girls who had wanted Varsity and not made it. There was Susan Yardley, sweet as a chickadee at the bird feeder — chirping and warm and delightful — but Susan's lovely personality hadn't matched the competition from gymnasts like Olivia and Nancy. There was Vanessa, one of the most striking human beings Mary Ellen had ever seen off television (and with her father the superintendent of schools — powerful, too) but Vanessa had not made it in spite of her looks and her father.

Vanessa did not see Mary Ellen. This afternoon Vanessa had eyes only for Pres. Pres, telling Angie that her weak shoulders meant he had better carry her out to his Porsche, did not notice Vanessa's glare in his direction.

Mary Ellen knew exactly how Vanessa was reacting, because Mary Ellen would have done the same. *How dare you not notice me!* she would be thinking. Of all the sins you have committed, Pres, the sin of not noticing me is worst. I demand to be seen. Disliked, maybe. But never, never, *never* ignored!

Mary Ellen smiled to herself and the movement of her lips set off yet another yawn. Next to her Troy said mildly, "What's keeping you up so late, Mary Ellen? Terrific movies on HBO?"

Mary Ellen blushed. Her family did not have cable TV, let alone HBO. Yawns were as embarrassing as hiccups. Worse, because people began wondering. With hiccups, they just laughed at you.

Troy's own technique was the best defense — no answer at all. Sweetly, Mary Ellen responded, "Do you go over to Pres's house very often, Troy?"

He accepted it without a flicker. "Not really. His mother isn't all that eager to have people in the house. It's odd, when you consider the place was built for entertaining. But when the Tilfords entertain, it's usually at the Country Club. Anyhow, Mrs. Tilford and Pres get on each other's nerves so much they can hardly co-exist these days."

"Then why are we being asked over there?" said Mary Ellen, as she and Troy walked to his car. She liked Mrs. Tilford. She would be perfectly happy to have a face, figure, marriage, and house like Mrs. Tilford.

"Probably because today is the day his mother works at the hospital," said Troy.

Mary Ellen slid across the seat, tucking her knees up to avoid the gear shift, and snuggled against Troy. Troy drove up Pres's drive with one hand, his right arm moving around Mary Ellen's shoulders. It took both of them to park the car, using Mary Ellen's right hand and Troy's left.

They were kissing each other before they even turned the engine off. Mary Ellen kissed Troy over and over, lightly, possessively, loving the response of his lips. In spite of being in such a public place, they had no audience. Everyone else was watching Olivia.

At first, Olivia had seemed aloof, almost unfriendly, and the squad was anxious about her. But the combination of cheerleading, and the forced intimacy of the squad had opened Olivia up enough so that she was able to enjoy the company of a boy for the first time in her life — and *that* had changed her personality even more.

"I cannot walk another inch," Olivia informed her boyfriend. Michael Barnes was a track star, long, lean, and tan even at this time of year in the north country. "Guess I'd better carry you," he said.

He swung Olivia up like a duffel bag, tossed her upside down on his shoulder, and walked into the house nonchalantly. Olivia beat a steady tattoo on his backside. "This isn't what I meant!" she yelled. "I meant that you should get me a limousine so I could come up that driveway in the proper fashion!"

"You should make your explanations earlier on," said Michael, ignoring the drumming fists.

Mary Ellen and Troy left his car reluctantly and followed after all the rest. "Want me to carry you like that?" teased Troy.

"We're far too civilized for such idiocy," Mary Ellen said. They kissed again. Troy said, "I don't know, Mary Ellen. That kiss was pure primitive passion. Nothing civilized about it at all."

Mary Ellen thought she really had simulated passion down pat. For the only one who *really knew* what a loving Mary Ellen was like was Patrick.

She and Troy bantered easily, enjoying each other in a relaxed way for the first time.

In the front hall, Michael set Olivia down. He knew she was thrilled to be in this house. Olivia's house was solid and sturdy in a good, ordinary neighborhood. But Pres's house was simply wonderful. Even Michael felt a little excitement.

A sharply turning wide staircase, wrapped by ornately carved banisters, rose two stories in the large foyer. On the first flight there was a window seat and opposite that, a tiny curved balcony. Fresh flowers sat in a china vase on a narrow pedestal, their bright colors gleaming down at the cheerleaders. Carved ceilings and an umbrella stand of intricately laced wood caught the eye, and as soon as they turned, they caught their own reflections in a mirror of dozens and dozens of diamond points.

"Oooh, look," whispered Olivia to Michael.

Olivia laughed with delight, and Michael grinned, enjoying her enjoyment. "It's like a movie set," he said to her.

"And this is just the foyer," she said.

But Pres did not offer a tour of the house, though they lingered by the stairs, half hoping. He led them through a wide gallery and down shallow steps covered with a wine-red runner and into the new addition most of them had seen when swimming in the lake. Great glass windows framed an immense family room off the remodeled kitchen.

It had a view of the lake as beautiful as they had ever seen. From here, it did not look as if there were more than a handful of other inhabited places on the whole lake. You could sit in the wonderful comfort of this room of red leather and deep carpet, warming your toes in front of the stone fireplace, and stare out at a scene much like what the first settlers must have enjoyed.

In much more comfort, too. No drafts.

Troy, with easy familiarity, got chips, fruit, and sodas out of one of the two refrigerators in the kitchen. Mary Ellen, helping him, saw that not only were the fridges full, but they were full of expensive things — Brie cheese, Heineken beer, artichokes, and honeydew melon out of season. Oh, to be wealthy! she thought.

70

She touched her two pieces of jewelry. It was her start. Like the investor with his first shares of stock. *This* was her beginning. She would have a house like this one day, too. Maybe not this very house, and maybe not Pres — but she would be rich and comfortable, she knew it.

Nancy's boyfriend Alex was not around. He worked Tuesdays. Nancy sat with Walt on one of the huge, soft sofas that lined the glass walls. Alex was rehearsing with his rock group, and she wished he could see this house.

"Walt?" she said.

"Mmmm?"

"I have to talk to you. Seriously."

He smiled at her and waited.

"I've heard the most awful rumor. I don't know what to do about it."

"What is it?" Walt asked.

"Everybody is talking about Mary Ellen. They're saying she's a shoplifter. That that's how she got the jewelry and new clothes."

Walt Manners ceased to breathe. *Mary Ellen?* His parents were going to principals, police, and students, *and it was Mary Ellen?* He stared across the room at their golden girl. She was leaning on the bar next to Troy, and her long, lovely fingers were entwined in the new gold necklace.

"Walt, do you think it can be true?" Nancy said.

Walt's parents had done a thousand interviews in his presence. He considered himself a fairly good judge of character. Now his first thought was not so much of Mary Ellen as of Nancy. Was

71

she seriously worried — or simply very eager to gossip? But one look at her anxiety, at the way she was biting her lips, convinced him. Nancy Goldstein was afraid. Afraid it was true, afraid to think about the ramifications of the truth.

Walt looked back at Mary Ellen. So happy, so lovely, so flawless.

And so poor.

Mary Ellen hated being poor.

Mary Ellen's clothing came from the Thrift Shop. He knew, because his mother went through clothes like a knife through cake; she had to have new, interesting outfits all the time so the viewers wouldn't be bored — and off to the Thrift Shop the clothing went. And sometimes the clothing that had graced his mother's ordinary, lean figure showed up a month later on Mary Ellen's slender, lovely young body.

Walt said heavily, "I don't know, Nancy. I truly don't know."

Nancy and Walt stared at each other, their expressions a mirror image. They both felt and looked sick.

But the room filled with happy activity, oblivious to the ugly topic that Nancy had quietly introduced to Walt, whom she instinctively trusted. Andrew and Kerry, surprised and delighted to be included yet again, were curling up on the couch next to Nancy. Angie was bouncing in with a diet drink in her hand, her fear of calories as usual her favorite topic of conversation.

Angie said, "What vicious, unkind person put the sour cream dip next to me?"

"The sour cream dip was here first," Walt told her. "But since I am the kindest person of all, I will remove it from your reach."

"First let me have just one taco chip," said Angie, and she scooped a huge pillow of white dip onto a tiny corner of taco chip. She giggled while they laughed at her.

I can't talk to Angie about the rumor, Nancy thought. Angie has probably never had an ugly thought about another human being in her life. She'd be shocked that I would even think of repeating such a thing.

Mary Ellen perched on the back of the sofa and leaned way over Nancy's shoulder to grab a few chips as Walt took them away.

How tired she looks, Nancy thought. Circles under her eyes. Mary Ellen? To whom appearance is everything?

What's she staying up late for? Perhaps it's not that she's staying up late — it's just that she can't fall asleep. Maybe it's worry. Shame. Fear of being caught.

And she *will* be caught, Nancy thought, wearing that necklace so openly. Anyone who shops in Tarenton knows it was in Marnie's window all month.

Nancy turned away, caught in revulsion at the idea that Mary Ellen would steal. For no reason except to fill a silence she found terrifying, Nancy said, "Angie, did you get a new lipstick? Can I try it?"

"Sure. It's a terrific color. Too light for you though, Nancy. You can get away with really brilliant colors. If I do that I'm nothing but a big gash of lips in a little teeny face. But try it." Angie handed Nancy her purse. Nancy began rifling through the purse, looking for the lipstick, which of course lay on the bottom.

All of them but Olivia, Andrew, and Kerry were taking European history and suffering from exam fears. "Well," said Pres, "ready for that big test Friday? It's the essay questions that worry me. Two hundred years of Europe? He could ask anything. You could study for weeks and not know the right topics."

Walt said, "At least the essays are take-home. It's the fill-in-the-blanks I hate. Without fail, the blanks are going to be the dates and the treaties and the kings I forgot."

"The essay is take-home?" Pres echoed. "I didn't know that! When did he announce that?"

Nancy thought she found the lipstick. She lifted a tiny, hard object but it was a miniature notebook. The size of return address stickers. It stuck in the palm of her hand and when she flicked at it with her opposite finger to make it fall back into Angie's purse, it opened.

In the tiniest penciled print she had ever seen, it said, "Kaiser Wilhelm I — 1871."

With her fingernail, she turned a page.

"Bismarck — Iron Chancellor — Triple Alliance."

Page after tiny page was filled with names and dates.

The tiny notebook fell out of Nancy's hand and into the bottom of Angie's purse.

It was a carefully made cheat book. One so tiny it would easily fit in the curve of a palm. Nancy could hardly think. But it was there in Angie's purse.

Kerry said, "I'm so glad I don't have to take that stuff. It sounds awful."

"You *do* have to take it," Pres said. "Senior year. If you plan to go to college."

"All those dates," Angie said. "They're really awful."

Nancy said quietly, "But you've learned them, haven't you, Angie?"

"Most of them," Angie said happily. "I don't know why, but things just fell into place for me this year. Usually I have trouble with academic subjects, but this is the best year of my life. Good grades, good squad, and a *perfect* man."

They all laughed at her inflection. *Perfect* man. The phrase resounded in the ears of each boy, all wanting to be described that way by some girl. *Perfect* man. Resounding, too, in the ears of each girl, yearning to find him.

Nancy excused herself and walked stiffly to the powder room. She must not look as rotten as she felt or somebody would have run after her to offer help. *Angie.* Was Angie cheating? Sweet, good, darling, decent Angie. *Cheating?* But she *had* made the honor roll. Unlikely for Angie — how had she done it?

Nancy got to the powder room, thinking she really, truly would throw up. She even knelt in front of the toilet and waited, but the nausea passed. After a while, feeling silly, she turned to

75

the sink and washed her hands for something to do.

She felt betrayed.

Her wonderful squad.

All these kids. Tarenton's finest.

And one of them was a shoplifter.

And one of them cheated.

And *those* were the ones least likely to be suspected of doing *anything* bad! God only knew what Pres and Walt and Olivia might be doing that Nancy wasn't aware of.

Oh, please God, let this be a nightmare, Nancy thought. Cheerleading is the best thing that's happened to me since I moved to Tarenton. I can't bear it if it's ruined. *I can't bear it.*

Hot, angry tears stung her eyes and she wiped them away at once. If it turns out to be true, she thought, I'm quitting the squad. But, no — I can't quit. People will think I'm just as bad if I quit; they'll figure I'm into something bad, too. I'll *have* to stay on!

She could not bear to be around her squad any longer. All that laughter and light, hiding the things they had done. She used the front hall telephone in its own clever niche by the umbrella stand. "Mother," she said into it urgently, "come and get me. *Now.*"

CHAPTER

Wednesday's game was the tensest they had ever cheered for. Wickfield scored four baskets and three foul shots in the first quarter, while Tarenton, the former champions, managed only two baskets total. The hateful score gleamed red at them from the lit-up scoreboards in each corner of the gym.

The squad felt stupid, cheering things like, *If you tangle with us, you fall,* and, *We're number one,* when the opposite team was winning by such a landslide.

Ardith drew her cheerleaders into a huddle. Very softly she said, "You must *not* forget whose side you're on. Our team isn't the enemy. You're angry at them for not doing as well as they usually do. They can feel that, you know. *You* are the support here. Let their coach yell *at* them. You yell *with* them."

Ardith sat back down again and watched her

squad. There was something about her four girls and two boys that was making her nervous. She could not pinpoint the trouble. They were not behaving like the squad they were. They were hardly even working together. Even physically, all six were keeping a distance from one another, as if this was the first day of practice and they were awkward strangers.

Why wasn't Mary Ellen, as captain, pulling everybody together? Why was the squad so unresponsive? So mechanical?

There was a light tapping on her shoulder. Ardith Engborg turned a little irritably because she hated being interrupted with a game and the cheers on her mind, but it was the principal, Mrs. Oetjen. There were few women Ardith respected more. She smiled at Mrs. Oetjen, but for the first time since she could remember, got no smile in return.

"I need to talk to you. Soon. When can we have some time together privately?" the principal asked. "It's urgent."

Ardith's stomach knotted. Something had to be radically wrong for Mrs. Oetjen to make such a request right during the basketball action. Olivia's health? Angie or Walt failing a subject?

But one look at the troubled eyes of the high school principal told Ardith Engborg that there was much more serious trouble out there. Could it be Pres? The hard, physical work of cheering had helped Pres immensely, siphoning off his anger and boredom. But it had unfortunately increased his parents' anger. Not only were they opposed to their son cheerleading, but cheerleading was taking up the hours they wanted to have Pres working at Tarenton Fabricators.

Pres was on edge.

Could he have done something criminal? The thought shocked Ardith, but it was not impossible. She tried to imagine what Pres might have done. His car came to mind. The car he loved so much and drove too fast and cornered too daringly.

Hit and run? Ardith thought, sick with anxiety. "Now is fine," she said. "Let's go to the teachers' lounge."

The principal nodded gravely. Ardith whispered to Mary Ellen to take complete charge and she'd be back shortly. Mary Ellen, eyes riveted to the team on the court, nodded abstractedly. What a relief to have a girl like Mary Ellen in control! She might not be able to stir the kids up tonight, but she was utterly reliable, utterly loyal to cheerleading and the squad.

Ardith and Mrs. Oetjen slipped out of the gym, passing in front of the stacked bleachers. The game was so demanding that almost no one in the audience saw the two women.

In the teachers' lounge Mrs. Oetjen insisted on making coffee, which increased Ardith's nervousness immensely, waiting for the measuring, the perking, the pouring, and the adding of sugar. Whatever is wrong, Ardith thought, I will stand behind my kids. I am their coach. I won't let them down.

Mrs. Oetjen came right to the point. "Ardith,

rumor has it that Mary Ellen Kirkwood is shop-lifting."

Up in the risers, Kerry looked down at the cheerleading squad. Kerry was having great difficulty getting her thoughts straight. The problem was, of course, that they were not so much thoughts as flashes of desire that she could not deal with on a thinking level.

Andrew of course was warming the bench. He spent most of his time on the bench anyhow, but in a game going as badly as this, he would never get off. But Kerry's eyes were not on Andrew. They were on Pres. How thoughtful of him to be a cheerleader, so she could reasonably spend most of the game enjoying the sight of him.

Kerry had always adored Pres. (She and every girl in school, Kerry thought ruefully.) Pres had a high profile. It was not just that he was from a first family of Tarenton, so to speak, and that he drove such a sexy car, but that his presence was so demanding: He walked, stood, and talked in such a way that very few girls could resist him. It had been true since Pres was a child and it was even truer now.

When Pres had first touched her, opened his car door for her, waved at her to signal her, he had been for Kerry like a wonderful but distant big brother finally deigning to bother with a kid sister. Clinging to Andrew, Kerry had been in awe of Pres, adoring him from afar.

But last night, at Pres's house, when Andrew was outside helping one of the other girls get her car started, Pres had led Kerry out of the big, red leather and plush carpeted room, through the impressive glossy kitchen, and into a tiny, cozy TV room. It had no views. It was an intimate, utterly comfortable little room where a family would curl up to watch late night movies together.

They sat on a loveseat: a couch built for two, its soft cushions dumping them closer to each other than a wider couch would have done. Pres talked of school and Kerry talked of school, and something rose between them that had nothing to do with school at all.

Desire.

Kerry got up quickly and walked in a circle, unsure of what to do about her feelings except that she'd better hide them from Pres, who would laugh at this little, plain sophomore with her pointless crush on him. But looking back at Pres, she could not even remember Andrew; she could only stare at Pres. Pres got up, too, and suddenly his arms were around her and they were kissing in a way she and Andrew had never kissed. A kiss that blotted out the rest of the world — all sounds, all thoughts. A kiss that made Preston Tilford the sum total of Kerry's existence.

The kiss lasted forever, and yet ended instantly.

Kerry was shaking.

Very lightly, very swiftly, they kissed several more times.

Then Andrew's voice pealed through the house. "Kerry?" he shouted. "Ready to go? My mom's here to get us. Angie's waiting. Come on!"

Kerry and Pres said nothing to each other.

Kerry's hand went to her fluffy hair to smooth it, but that was useless: Her hair was always fly-away and there was nothing to smooth. It was a gesture to keep herself from wrapping her arms around Pres again. Kerry turned and literally fled down the hall, bumping into Andrew in the kitchen. Andrew noticed nothing unusual about her. He handed her her coat and told her how cold it was outside, and how lucky his mom had been to get that car started.

Kerry barely heard him. She saw him now as an ordinary, dull boy with a mildly attractive personality — nothing next to the star that was Pres. It horrified her. What kind of way was that to think of the boy who had dated her all these months and been such a delight to her?

Kerry did not sleep well that night. Nothing like this had ever happened to her. A churning of her blood and nerves woke her almost hourly. She was consumed with the thought of this one male human being.

And now, tonight, watching Pres cheer, catching his eyes now and then, Kerry was completely confused.

Pres was one to enjoy himself with any girl . . . with all girls. Usually he dated the splashy, impressive ones: Mary Ellen Kirkwood, Vanessa Barlow. What on earth would make Pres Tilford, III, even glance in the direction of Kerry Elliot?

Once Kerry had to make up a poem about herself in English class. She could still remember how her rhyme had gone. How easily it came to her, and once written, how painfully apt.

> Kerry . . .
> . . . very . . .
> Ordinary.

Maybe he just wants sex, she thought. His kiss said something. I don't have much experience. I'm sure he has plenty. Did he figure I'd be easy to get in the first place, then easy to toss off when he's bored?

It was an unpleasant thought that should have made it easy to dismiss Pres from her mind, but instead he loomed larger. Pres's head moved very close to Angie, as their lithe bodies bent in a curve, and then rocketed in a leap. A few rows away, Vanessa Barlow stared at him, her beautiful lips curled in jealousy and anger. She must think Angie is a threat to her, Kerry thought. That's totally not true. Pres really is being a big brother to Angie. Anybody on the squad could tell Vanessa that.

What would Vanessa think if she had seen our kiss? Kerry thought. Would she think that I'm a threat to her, too?

It was truly funny. Kerry laughed aloud.

Little, ordinary Kerry. A threat to splendid, tawny, sultry Vanessa.

Kerry wondered if Pres would ask her out. But that was silly. Of course he wouldn't. He had just been temporarily swept up by an unexpected feeling. Now it was past.

Past for him, at least. Kerry was still swamped by her feelings. Did Vanessa feel the same?

On her left, one of Kerry's girl friends said, "Did you hear the rumor about Mary Ellen Kirkwood?"

All eyes flew to the beautiful golden girl they half idolized, half envied. Most of them wished for the beauty and agility cheerleading required, and most of them would have given anything to look like Mary Ellen Kirkwood.

"No. What?"

"She's shoplifting."

"That's ridiculous," said Kerry, not giving it a second thought. She watched the basketball team. At halftime, Tarenton was far behind. The team left the court dispiritedly and entered their locker room, where no doubt they would get the lecture of their lives from their disappointed coach.

Kerry tried to think of Andrew and his dismay and his needs, but there wasn't room for Andrew in her mind right now. Pres was taking up all the available space.

With Andrew out of sight, Kerry felt much less guilty. Her friends vanished, clambering down row after row of risers, to get popcorn and soft drinks in the foyer. Kerry rested her hands on her chin, leaned her elbows on her knees, and watched the halftime show of the Tarenton Varsity Squad.

Oh, Pres, she thought.

Pres and Walt were lifting each girl by turns, so that the floor cheer resembled a dance, flashing scarlet, the music on the tapes resounding from every corner. Kerry's heart beat as loudly as the drums.

Patrick Henley went out of doors during half-time. One reason he liked his work and stuck it out in spite of the endless ribbing he got from so many of the kids was that he hated being cooped up inside — especially in cold weather, when thermostats were turned up and you sweated and the air turned musty. Then he was trapped by the walls and could hardly endure school or anything else that kept him in one place.

He lounged by the wide, shallow steps, thinking of Mary Ellen the way he always had to think of her now — distantly. Like some sort of movie star you never actually met, but had posters of on your walls. He had kissed Mary Ellen, and she had kissed him with great ardor; they had shared classes and lunch tables — and years ago school buses. But Mary Ellen had kept her distance and he knew why.

Snobbery. Pure snobbery.

Two feet away, a pair of boys from Wickfield were discussing the game. Patrick was an avid Tarenton fan, but there was no way to pretend that Tarenton was playing a decent game tonight. Tonight stank. Still, he felt resentment building toward Wickfield in general.

One of the Wickfield boys said, "And you heard about that cheerleader, didn't you?"

"Which one?"

"The blonde one you had a crush on last year. The one who wouldn't even *talk* to anybody from Wickfield."

Patrick grinned. That sounded like Mary Ellen.

"The one who ought to be a magazine centerfold?" said the other boy.

"You got it. Well, I heard from a kid at Tarenton High, who ought to know, that she's a shoplifter."

"*Mary Ellen?* The beautiful blonde?" The boy with the crush on Mary Ellen was shocked.

But he wasn't half as shocked as Patrick Henley. Patrick stood almost frozen, staring at Mary Ellen's accuser. Rage rose inside him.

"I got it on good authority," said the kid. "She's a shoplifter. Steals all the time — jewelry, perfume, clothes. Kind of a hobby, I guess."

Patrick grabbed the Wickfield kid by the shoulders and spun him around hard. Anger for Mary Ellen was rushing through him like an electrical charge. Accusing the girl he adored of stealing! Spreading some damn rumor that Mary Ellen — *his Mary Ellen!* — was a common thief!

Patrick Henley was no lightweight. When his fist connected with the Wickfield kid's jaw, the boy staggered backward. But the steps were crowded with people taking in the fresh air and talking. And at a volatile high school game, filled with traditional rivalries, there were always police. Patrick had barely drawn back his arm a second time than the police were yelling.

Patrick swung anyway.

In moments there were a half dozen people

fighting: Patrick and *only* Patrick from Tarenton, the rest from Wickfield. Nobody except Patrick had any idea why they were fighting . . . and nobody except Patrick cared.

The two cops shoved into the melee.

They weren't as rough as the boys, and not a fraction as rough as Patrick, but their uniforms were obvious even in the half light of the building's shadow. Most of the Wickfield boys stopped immediately. The cops grabbed Patrick by the jacket and shoved him backward against the brick walls that lined the steps.

"Henley?" said one in absolute astonishment. "Don't you have that garbage route?" They weren't used to dealing with the good kids, the hard-working kids. Patrick knew they would give him the benefit of the doubt. The cop said, "It's just a basketball game, kid. Sometimes we lose, right?"

Patrick nodded. He looked at his fist. The knuckles were bloody. Mary Ellen would love it. Boys fighting over her. She'd think it was the most exciting thing she'd ever heard.

But he could never tell her, and if word got around that he'd been fighting, he could never say why. He could never repeat that rumor himself. *Mary Ellen shoplifting.* The thought made him furious all over again, and as he faced the Wickfield kid again, the cops tensed beside him, feeling his anger.

"You hurt bad?" one of the Wickfield kids said to his friend.

The boy massaged his jaw and looked hard at

87

Patrick. The depth of Patrick's anger reached him, and he figured out why he'd been hit. Not because Wickfield was scoring baskets, that was for sure.

He figures I'm her boyfriend, Patrick thought, glaring right back. Close enough. It'll shut him up anyway.

"I'm all right," said the Wickfield boy. "Let's just forget about it."

The Wickfield boys went inside. The last thing the police wanted was a war on a night like this, so they stayed with Patrick and kidded him about some of the dumps on his garbage route, and how they had a feeling there were certainly places where he purposely made the truck backfire. Then they gave him a little lecture he didn't listen to and suggested that he skip the rest of the game.

Good advice, Patrick thought, who normally hated any advice, good or bad.

If he went back into that steaming, body-packed gymnasium, and saw Mary Ellen and her lovely smile — Mary Ellen, totally ignorant of what was being said — and then he looked back at the Wickfield crowd. . . . Well, it was better *not* to go back.

He said to the police, "Sorry about that."

"Hey, listen. Happens to all of us. Just keep the old lid on, kid."

Patrick nodded. He walked across the school lawns to the parking lot, the rumor staying in his head no matter how much he wanted it to go. A reliable source, they'd said. Someone from Tarenton. And who, just *who* at Tarenton High, would spread a rotten rumor like that about Mary Ellen Kirkwood?

Inside the gym, Varsity finished up its floor routines just as the basketball team returned for its warmups. The six cheerleaders ran clapping off the floor, and took a moment's rest on the sidelines. They sipped water, relaxed slightly, exchanged theories on how well the third quarter would go.

"Okay," said Mary Ellen, getting up and motioning them to follow her. "Sideline cheers. The name sequence."

They started the unison clapping, reciting the names and numbers of team members, that would rebuild the excitement so that at the moment the game was launched, the crowd would be back at a fever pitch.

Ardith Engborg came back into the gym. Heavily she climbed over one riser to sit behind her squad. She clapped with them, setting an example, but her smile of pride was forced.

Mary Ellen continued to give orders, so that the squad turned partially time and again, their voices directed to different parts of the gym. Pres counted the turns until he was facing Kerry again, and he looked right at her. She waved her fingers at him. He wanted to put his hands under his chin, cupping them the way she had hers, but he didn't dare imitate her; Mary Ellen and Ardith would be furious if he broke pattern.

The score was 29 to 11. Bad, but basketball was a fast game. That could easily be reversed in the next two quarters.

The game began once more.

Wickfield's team was delirious with the prospect of whipping last year's champions on their home turf. Tarenton fans were upset at being so far behind, an experience they didn't often have in basketball. This third quarter, both teams played well and fiercely. All the fans cheered themselves hoarse.

For once, the Varsity Squad was almost unnecessary. Nobody needed encouragement to yell. In fact, at this game, the danger was in yelling too much! Word had gotten around that there had been some fighting outside, and as tension mounted, a fighting feeling possessed the whole gym.

As Tarenton narrowed the gap, and it became clear they had an excellent chance of surpassing Wickfield after all, the fans began screaming at the referees over every single decision. The poor referees could do nothing right. For every foul they called, the fans felt they missed five.

Mary Ellen had to drown out loud, unpleasant remarks. She ordered the squad to start the Answer cheer. This could be counted on to absorb even the most hostile crowd.

"Who do we love?" she screamed with her crew, using her large white megaphone with its bright red T.

"Tarenton!"

"Who's gonna win?" Varsity bellowed.

"Tarenton!"

"How do you spell it?" Varsity asked at the top of their lungs.

Momentarily this worked, but then Troy fouled out of the game. He had to go to the bench for good. Tarenton fans were furious at a decision they felt was unfair. Mary Ellen led the Yea, rah-rah, *Troy!* cheer, but it only increased the wrath of those who felt Tarenton couldn't win without Troy.

Mary Ellen grieved for Troy, but dismissed him from her mind quickly. Cheering came first. She faced the several hundred anxious fans and yelled, "Give me a T!"

"*T!*"

"Give me an *A!*"

She was glad "Tarenton" was a fairly long word to spell. By the time they'd finished screaming out the letters, and agreed:

"What does it spell?"
"*TARENTON!*"

the game was back in high gear again.

The score was even at last.

Screams ricocheted off the walls of the gym.

Two minutes were left in the game. But anything could happen in two minutes. No one could begin to predict who would win the game. Each side was fiercely determined to have the next score. The crowd was on its feet, unable to bear the tension from a sitting position. The cheerleaders, for all their bright Tarenton red, or gaudy Wickfield green, were invisible and inaudible.

And then both Paul Bergman and Peter Stolle, Tarenton's finest seniors, fouled out.

91

Tarenton could not believe it.

"Miss, miss, miss!" they screamed at the Wickfield boys taking foul shots. The pressure was so great that all four shots were missed. Wickfield shouted its displeasure, Tarenton its joy, and the referees caught it all around.

Every single senior on the Tarenton team was now on the bench for good. All that experience, all that height — benchwarming. The fans sagged with dismay, realizing that there was no way they could win now. There was nobody to substitute at this point but a bunch of inexperienced, short, slim sophomores. And to be put on the court at this moment with all this tension could only spell failure.

The coach put Andrew Poletti into the game.

For Angie's sake, the Varsity Squad flung itself into cheers of pride over Andrew. They didn't believe in him, but they *sounded* as if they believed in him, and they convinced the crowd. Angie's leaps had never been higher and her voice never stronger. She *did* believe in her brother. *Completely*.

Nine seconds before the end of the game, Andrew made a basket, breaking the tie and putting Tarenton ahead by two. Into the din and chaos of the screaming hundreds of fans, Wickfield took the ball, raced down the floor and with three seconds left and nothing to lose, tried a too distant shot . . .

And missed.

The final game bell was drowned out by the screaming, stomping joy of a last moment Tarenton victory. Andrew was crushed in a huddle of triumphant basketball players. The cheerleading squad was laughing, clapping, screaming, and hugging Angie.

Ardith Engborg, stomach churning with ulcerating distress, waited for the joy to calm before approaching Mary Ellen.

Andrew won it all, Pres Tilford thought. Right in front of Kerry. What can I do to match that? Nothing. He'll be the king of Kerry's court.

As for Kerry, she did not dare look at Pres. Andrew's most exciting moment, and he might catch his girl adoring another boy? It was unthinkable.

How could she ever make it through the victory party? They would all go to Kenny's Pizza; this much was traditional. Pres would be there, in the midst of the Varsity Squad. In fact, Pres would probably escort Angie, and Angie and Pres would certainly sit with Andrew. And Kerry would have to sit facing Pres, two feet away from the boy whose clothes she felt like ripping off, and pretend that she was having a wonderful time with Andrew.

Talk about self-control.

CHAPTER

7

"But I hate onions," Nancy Goldstein wailed.

Huge wedges of pizza moved around the two booths the cheerleaders had taken in the back of Kenny's Pizza. "You have to eat your onions," said Alex. "When I kiss you, I don't want you to tell me *I* have onion breath."

"Who wants my pepperoni?" Olivia said.

Everybody wanted her pepperoni. They all lunged for it and Walt got mozzarella on his elbow.

Waitresses circulated with napkins and pitchers of Coke. The kids ate from each other's slices. Oozing hot pizza went into hungry mouths and ice cubes clinked in empty glasses.

Nancy was not eating. She had arms and lips wrapped around Alex. Alex had decided not to have pizza after all and was trying to convince the waitress to bring him a dish of spaghetti. The waitress was having difficulty understanding his request since Nancy's mouth was blocking Alex's.

They were all laughing, swept up in the wonderful high of victory when all had seemed lost. They talked too loud, ate too much, laughed uproariously.

Walt Manners said to Nancy, "Where's Mary Ellen?"

Alex said, "I haven't seen her."

Nancy looked around, surprised. How could Mary Ellen, their captain, not be at the celebration? Mary Ellen loved parties. "I don't know where she is," Nancy said. "How odd. She and Troy must have gone somewhere else." But it didn't sound like Mary Ellen. Mary Ellen was too much of a party girl to pass one up.

"Troy just came in alone," Walt said.

He and Nancy looked at each other, their laughter dwindling.

"Sounds sinister," Alex said. "Maybe old Troy did away with Mary Ellen."

Nancy giggled. It was sort of silly to worry about Mary Ellen. She was seventeen years old. If she got stranded, she was perfectly capable of using a telephone to rescue herself. Nancy glanced at Troy. He sat with a group of kids who were already jammed into a booth. He certainly wasn't leaving any room for somebody else to sit with him. Troy and Melon had a fight, Nancy thought. Poor girl. She's not having the terrific year she thought she would.

Alex was talking to Nancy, and she turned back to him. What fine features Alex had! Nancy looked into his eyes, eyes that had seemed crazy and wild to her when she first met Alex, but now seemed both loving and understanding. Even his earring didn't put her off anymore.

Alex was not fond of Mary Ellen, who he said was a snob with nothing to be a snob about. When Alex heard the rumors about Mary Ellen shoplifting, he merely said he wasn't surprised. Nancy defended Mary Ellen, but they hadn't talked about it long. Alex wasn't interested.

She'll have to take care of herself, Nancy decided. She turned her thoughts to Alex again. It was easy to do.

Two tables away, Kerry sat wrapped in Andrew's arms. It was not what she had in mind, but Andrew was so excited and so proud of himself that he literally could not keep still. Andrew was hugging her constantly, as if extra adrenalin kept surfacing and hugs helped release it. Every few minutes, remembering his brilliant score, he'd laugh breathlessly, and kiss whatever part of Kerry was closest to him.

Here I am, she thought, in the arms of the basketball star, every girl's dream . . . and I want to be somewhere else.

Pres never took his eyes off her.

Kerry was more aware of Pres's constant gaze than Andrew's constant embrace. Her skin was flushed. It was partly that the press of bodies had raised the temperature in the pizza house, and partly the excitement and thrill of the evening. But it was mostly the effect of Pres's unblinking attention.

Nobody noticed. Kerry always looked pink-cheeked and scatterbrained. Tonight she was just more so.

Pres sent her messages with his eyes. She was not sure how to interpret them. She merely stared back.

The already dim light of Kenny's Pizza was suddenly blocked and their booth turned dark as the shadow of a man — a big man — was cast over their table. Kerry, startled, looked up to see the man cup hands over his mouth and very loudly imitate a trumpet call. "Ta da da daaaaa!" he blew. Man's crazy, Kerry thought. Who on earth is he?

"Marc!" shrieked Angie.

Angie climbed out of the back of their booth, without giving anybody time to slide out for her, stood right on Pres's thigh, took a dangerous step on the rickety table, missed the last pizza wedge by a quarter inch, and lurched toward Marc.

They're both crazy, Kerry thought. But she loved the way Angie's face had lit up and the way Marc was laughing as he reached for her. Pres boosted Angie forward by the ankle, Marc caught his girl in his arms, and the whole back end of the pizza house gave them a round of applause.

"I didn't know you were coming!" Angie cried, kissing him with such vigor that Kerry wanted the same from Pres. Evidently hers was a widespread feeling — all the kids whistled and clapped. Angie, who had stage presence to spare, bowed sweepingly, waving at her fans and agreeing that her kisses were the equal of her cheerleading splits — spectacular.

"I'm going to stay over," Marc said. "I made arrangements to avoid class tomorrow morning."

Pres laughed. "Why don't you just say you're cutting?"

"You shouldn't cut class," Angie said.

"Go on," Marc said. "You love it. I sacrificed for you, Angie. Drove all this way and scoured the town to find the celebration. Tell me you're not thrilled."

"I'm thrilled."

Marc grinned. He reached over Pres to grab Angie's coat, tucked her into it, waved at them all in a general sort of way, and escorted Angie out of Kenny's Pizza.

Now there were three at the table: Kerry and Andrew on one side, Pres alone on the other.

Pres Tilford was not one to waste time. Running his long fingers through his blond hair, he said to Andrew, "There's the reporter from the local paper. He didn't get to talk to you after the game, did he? Go on over to him. Give the guy an interview."

"Yes," Kerry said, feeling half like Andrew's ally and half like his enemy. "Do it, Andrew."

Andrew left them.

They were alone now. Eyes like magnets, hearts beating to match their excitement.

"How steady are you going with Andrew?" Pres said first.

How seriously he said this! Could Kerry trust him? What if she dumped Andrew for Pres, only to be dumped by Pres in a week? It would certainly be in keeping with Pres's social history.

How do you know? Kerry thought. How do you tell love from passing interest? "Not very steady. Off and on for a month or so."

Pres's beautiful features relaxed slightly. Or was she kidding herself? Pres — anxious about the answer of an ordinary sophomore? "Good," Pres said. "Will you go out with me Friday?"

"Yes."

Kerry had never had a conversation with a boy who was so direct. And yet, they were doing nothing but flirting. It was a classic case. As Pres turned his head slightly to offer his profile, she tossed her hair. As she pursed her lips in a mock kiss, his ankle brushed against hers.

I'm going to be sorry for this, she thought.

But Pres was too handsome, too desirable, for her to worry too much. No wonder the girls fell for him! To think that after Mary Ellen and Vanessa and girls like that, he would ask me out, she thought.

"I don't know what to tell Andrew," she said. How sexy Pres's dark brown eyes were under that shock of blond hair. His eyebrows weren't the color of either his hair or eyes, but had a personality of their own.

"That you don't want to be tied down," Pres said. "It's a standard line. I hear it a lot."

"You also *use* it a lot," Kerry said dryly.

"Not with you," Pres said.

Their eyes lost the locked grip. Both suddenly self-conscious, they looked down at the pizza remains, which were safe. Kerry found herself cleaning up used napkins and Pres found himself signaling for more Coke.

Back at Tarenton High School, in the locker room, Ardith Engborg stood looking at the most dedicated squad captain she had ever coached.

Hair flowing around her shoulders, Mary Ellen's face was framed in soft tendrils. Her perfect complexion was rosy from the game's exertion, and cornflower blue eyes sparkled from the joy of victory. The cheerleading uniform became Mary Ellen wonderfully: On her the scarlet and white were dashing, exciting.

Ardith Engborg felt physically ill. Could this beautiful, good girl be a shoplifter? Could Mary Ellen, whose plans were so firm, whose future was so well thought out, have jeopardized everything for the sake of a few sweaters and necklaces?

Half bouncing, half laughing, Mary Ellen called over her shoulder, "Be right with you, Troy. Ardith wants to talk to me for a moment."

Troy, Ardith thought. Mary Ellen certainly knows how to pick them. "Mrs. Engborg," she corrected Mary Ellen gently. It would not be good to start *this* interview with the intimacy of her own first name.

Mary Ellen was startled. "I'm sorry," she said. The kids all referred to their coach as Ardith and she hadn't thought before speaking. But if there was any guilt in her, Mrs. Engborg could not see it. She could see only a lovely seventeen-year-old cheerleader, barely able to contain herself until she could be with that handsome eighteen-year-old boy.

"I'll wait," called Troy. "I'll be in the gym."

Ardith Engborg walked back between the rows of lockers to be sure that she and Mary Ellen were alone in the locker room. Then she shut the door to the gym. Troy's shadow disappeared as if he were being swallowed up. The door closed softly, but finally, with a thick thud. "The principal asked me to discuss a possible problem with you," Ardith said carefully.

"Oh? What's wrong?"

Ardith Engborg drew a deep breath, fortifying herself with oxygen. "Shoplifting has been a problem over at the mall lately. The managers of the department stores have spoken to Mrs. Oetjen about it. It seems to be a strong possibility, Mary Ellen, that you acquired your jewelry, clothing, and perfume by shoplifting.

Mary Ellen stared at her. *Shoplifting?*

"I am completely behind you, Mary Ellen." It was a coaching voice: firm, loving, expecting obedience and hard work. "I don't want you to feel I am accusing you of anything. But we need to know how you paid for what you're wearing these days."

If she had been standing on the San Andreas Fault during a major earthquake, Mary Ellen's world could not have shifted more. *"Shoplifting?"* she repeated. Her fingers groped in the air, found a locker handle, and held it until her knuckles were white. *"Me?"*

Ardith looked into her eyes. "Trust me, Mary Ellen. I'll help you, whatever it is. I'll stand by you."

If Ardith had phrased it any other way, Mary Ellen would not have gotten angry. But it sounded as if the coach already believed her cheerleader was a thief. As if Ardith just wanted Mary Ellen to admit it, so they could proceed with a trial. Mary Ellen was supposed to trust Mrs. Engborg, but Mrs. Engborg didn't trust her.

Shock turned to rage.

Trembling horror congealed into wrath.

How dare she? Mary Ellen thought. I am the best captain they've ever had in Tarenton. I work harder, I organize better. I am truly Varsity. How dare she stand there and believe that I'm a thief? How dare she not tell Mrs. Oetjen to take her suspicions somewhere else?

The Eismar twins. That day in Marnie's. That was why they had looked at her so strangely.

Rumors. Everybody in the school had listened to rumors. Everybody had spread rumors. They saw all Mary Ellen's lovely new things, and did they say how pretty she looked, how perfectly her accessories matched? No. They started calling her names. Shoplifter. Thief.

Mary Ellen wanted to wear boots with cleats and jump up and down on the bare flesh of everybody who had spread a rumor like that.

She looked at Mrs. Engborg, whom she had worshipped for years, and saw the woman in a new light. Someone willing to believe the worst about her. "I would never shoplift, Mrs. Engborg," Mary Ellen said steadily. "I would never steal. As to how I got the jewelry I have, *that* is my business. I resent the fact that you've even asked me. It's mine. I bought it. I won't discuss it anymore."

She, Mary Ellen, who had obeyed Ardith without question several days a week for two years — she was delivering the ultimatum. It amazed Mary Ellen only slightly less than being accused in the first place.

Mrs. Engborg opened her mouth to say something more, but Mary Ellen could not bear to hear another syllable. "Good-night, Mrs. Engborg," she said with forced courtesy. "I'll see you at practice tomorrow."

She took her coat and walked swiftly out of the locker room. The reaction set in the moment she pushed the door open and saw Troy standing there. She had forgotten Troy. *Had he heard?*

Mary Ellen's knees turned to jelly. Her hands went so clammy and damp she could not pull her mittens on over them. Her skin stuck to the wool. Troy did not smile at her. He did not put his arms around her and he didn't kiss her. He didn't help her on with her coat and he didn't slow his pace to walk with her out of the gym. "Everybody went to Kenny's for pizza," he said. "Let's catch up."

Everybody.

Everybody who had gossiped. Who had wondered.

She couldn't go. She couldn't sit there and laugh and clap and celebrate, when the world thought she was a thief.

They got to Troy's car. Troy busied himself with driving. She sat in the dark fighting the hot, stinging tears. Troy couldn't see her well. She pulled the hood of her ski jacket forward. Mary Ellen sat hidden by fake fur, while tears slipped down her cheeks.

Troy appeared to notice nothing.

I have to go home, Mary Ellen thought drearily. I can't possibly go for pizza.

With a tremendous effort Mary Ellen controlled her voice. "Troy, I'm really exhausted." Furtively, she wiped her cheeks dry. "I know how much fun it'll be at Kenny's, but I'm not up to it. I'm really sorry. You go, okay? Just drop me at home."

Troy's bland, unflappable voice said, "That's okay, Mary Ellen. Don't worry about it. You really threw yourself into the game and I can see how you'd be worn out. I'll see you in school tomorrow."

Was he being very understanding? Or had he rehearsed that in his mind, hoping he could get away from this girl suspected of stealing?

All that mattered was to get in the house without breaking down. She had shared the bedroom with Gemma from the day her younger sister was born, and she knew how to stifle sobs under a pillow without disturbing her sleeping sister.

"Good-night, Troy."

"Good-night, Mary Ellen."

Like a couple of sportscasters wrapping up the evening report. When Mary Ellen got out of the car, Troy didn't even put the car in park; he just waited for her to shut the door and then backed out of the driveway. For the first time she could remember, her own date didn't wait to see her safely inside her house.

Troy had not behaved that way on their other dates.

That meant he had heard Ardith's accusation. *And believed it.*

As Mary Ellen walked into her house, determined to last another five minutes in front of her parents, Vanessa Barlow was sitting in the pizza house with the Eismar twins and two boys from the basketball team. She didn't care for the ratio of boys to girls. Sharing two boys with two other girls? It was not Vanessa's style at all.

A glance across the room at her favorite boy, Pres Tilford, changed everything. Angie was leaving the room with Marc.

Whatever kind of crush Pres might have on Angie, Angie certainly didn't have one on Pres. She abandoned him with so many shrieks of delight, you would have thought Pres was carrying typhoid instead of a roll of ten-dollar bills. And then Andrew wandered off, and Pres was left there with plump, boring little Kerry what's-her-name.

Swiftly, Vanessa slid away from her group and crossed the restaurant to join Pres. She had a slinky walk. It was something she had studied and practiced. Vanessa was a naturally slinky person: like a jungle cat, everything about her was sinuous. She could not slip quietly over to Pres — she had to fling her long black hair about, attract as much attention as possible, and exchange a few insults with her favorite opponents.

Pres was sitting on the very outside of his booth. There was space for another person between him and the wall. Vanessa, without speaking either to Pres or Kerry, perched an inch of her curving rear end on the rim of Pres's bench and leaned backward onto his shoulders. Her thick dark hair spilled across his chest. Pres's fingers dipped into its masses. Vanessa laughed to herself. She loved her hair. There wasn't a boy in all Tarenton who didn't find all that thick black silk sexy.

She pressed against Pres to make him slide over the bench and give her room. Pres, as always, was difficult. Vanessa didn't mind. She enjoyed pitting her talents against his. Balancing herself, Vanessa prepared for one of the hot, charged arguments they usually had.

"Vannie," he said, using the nickname she *loathed*, "I'm busy right now. Mind sitting somewhere else?"

"Busy eating pizza? You'll get fat, Pres. Cheerleaders can't be fat. Especially preppy boy cheerleaders." She tilted her head way back and looked upside down at Pres. She could not tell, from the lines on his face, whether he was frowning or smiling. But he didn't move an inch and she was uncomfortable. It irritated Vanessa beyond mea-

106

sure that Pres would be uncooperative in front of this stupid little sophomore. Vanessa looked at Kerry. A little thick in the waist. Seven, eight pounds there she didn't need.

"Maybe I'd better eat your pizza for you," she said to Kerry. "You've got to start watching your figure." Vanessa paused. "In fact, darling, you should have started watching it freshman year."

Pres shifted to his left as if she were a soccer ball and he was hitting it with his hip. Vanessa fell straight onto the floor, hitting the base of her spine with an agonizing whack. Her sweater hooked on the back of the bench, pulling up to expose her skin, and she ripped a nasty scratch up her backbone.

"Sorry," said Pres.

The shock and humiliation were so great Vanessa would have kicked him if she'd been at the right angle.

"Oh, Vanessa!" cried Kerry. "Are you all right? Help her up, Pres. Are you hurt, Vanessa?"

Vanessa prepared herself to face the amusement of everybody watching, but when she flung back her hair to make a wise remark, she was shocked to see that nobody had noticed her. She, Vanessa, had made a fool of herself and nobody had so much as glanced her way. Laughing, eating, drinking, hugging — they couldn't care less whether Vanessa Barlow sat on the floor or the ceiling.

She had to cling to the rickety table to pull herself up, and it hurt. For a moment she wasn't sure she could straighten up all the way. Pres was saying to Kerry, "What do you think? Can we swallow more pizza or not?"

I'll kill him, Vanessa thought. He dates Mary Ellen to spite me, he flirts with Angie to spite me, now he's ordering pizza with this worthless little chubbette to spite me. I'll kill him.

She thought of an oil slick on a curve in the road above a convenient cliff, and Pres going too fast in his Porsche.

"Don't turn into the Loch Ness Monster on me, Vannie," Pres said. "Sorry I did that. You know how impulsive I am. You okay?"

"I'm fine," said Vanessa, looking down at the shiny blond hair that had briefly been hers to ruffle.

"You can sit with us if you *really* want to," Pres said.

"Pres!" Kerry said in rebuke of his rudeness.

Vanessa swung around so that her two feet of hair swirled out from her head like a black silk shawl, and went back to her old table.

"You're not very nice, Pres," Kerry said.

"I'm nicer than Vanessa."

Nobody could argue with that. Kerry laughed. She hadn't liked Vanessa commenting on her weight, especially in front of a splendid specimen of male like Pres Tilford. She kind of liked the way Pres had defeated Vanessa in one quick hiplash.

Kerry leaned across the table, hands supporting her chin. In precise imitation, Pres rested his chin in his palm and slid his elbows across the pockmarked tabletop until their elbows met and braced each other. His chin was higher than hers because his arms were long. Pres let his elbows slide outwards until his face was exactly even with Kerry's. They were approximately two inches apart.

Pres moved his cupped hands an inch farther forward.

Kerry, smothering a smile, did the same.

Their lips touched.

It wasn't a kiss. It was a feather-light brush of lip against lip.

They both retreated that inch and stared into each other's eyes.

"Once more with feeling," whispered Pres.

This time it was definitely a kiss. They lingered. Pres thought to himself, Cut. Enough. There's time. With Kerry, I'll have time. I'll *make* time.

He slid slowly backward, so the kiss didn't stop so much as fade away. Each leaned back, quarter inch by quarter inch, and when Andrew rejoined them they were still sitting there, chins in cupped hands, gazing at each other.

Andrew said, "Gee, I'm really sorry I deserted you for so long."

"That's okay," Pres said. "We had fun."

Marc Filanno didn't have many opportunities to enjoy his Angie. College was very difficult this semester. The drive from the campus to Tarenton was increasingly harder to make. He looked at this lovely girl, so aptly named Angela, and knew he'd been right to make the effort tonight. They had gone to a small coffee shop that the kids from Tarenton High rarely went to, so they had the privacy they wanted.

Angie was flushed with the excitement of a surprise victory, filled with pride because her brother had brought in the final two points. How proud Angie was of her family. Angie never spoke of her mother or brothers without complimenting them.

Marc wondered how Angie spoke of *him*. He'd never overheard such a conversation, but he figured he knew what it would be like. "Marc?" Angie would say. She would smile blissfully, with that open adoration that made him feel like a god. "Marc is perfect."

Angie promised him she'd visit the following weekend on the day there was no basketball game to cheer for. "I can't remember the schedule, Marc. It's either Friday or Saturday night that we're free. I'll call you."

"Okay. Do you have a pencil? I'll draw you a map to show you where I'm living now. It was too expensive living with just two other guys. I've moved. There are four of us now. Crowded, but cheap."

Angie fished in her handbag for a pencil. Marc waited patiently. Angie carried her entire universe in her purse. It generally took her five minutes to find anything. Marc never asked her for change when they drove on a toll road. Change purses fell to the bottom. Quarters were lost forever.

"Never mind the pencil," Marc said at last.

"I'll just tell you. Stop hunting and pay attention. It's confusing. Lots of one-way roads on that campus."

"No, no, no. I've got a pencil here somewhere, I know I do." Angie lost patience and upended her handbag on the table. Marc whisked his half-finished sandwich away just in time to avoid the flood of debris that poured out of the leather bag.

"I can never believe you really carry all that stuff around. I should think you'd get a backache from the weight," he told her.

Hairbrush, Kleenex packet, nail polish remover, calculator, box of earrings, bottle of aspirin, broken pencil, three lipsticks, whole pencil, assignment notebook. . . .

"I haven't cleaned house in ages," Angie remarked. "Look. Here's a tiny notebook I don't even remember. What on earth do I have this for?"

"What kind of housekeeper are you going to be when we get married?" Marc teased, tossing crumpled quiz papers and used Kleenex into a pile.

"Listen, buddy. When we get married, *you'll* be just as much of a housekeeper as I am. We'll be in lockstep. Every time *you* clean something, *I'll* clean something. Got it?"

Marc laughed. "Got it. What's the matter? Why are you frowning, Angie?"

She said, "Marc, this little book." She was turning white. Marc was shocked at her face. The warm, wonderful expression was being ironed away. Her lovely face grew tight and pinched.

111

"It's a cheat book. It's — why, it's dates and wars. Kings and treaties. It's for European history, Marc. It's . . . oh, Marc, Marc —" her voice grew as pinched as her face. Anxiously, frantically, she said, "I didn't make this, Marc."

He was astonished at her need to say that. "I know," he said reassuringly. "You'd never cheat." He took the little book out of her hands to examine it himself. "I just want to see if that's what it is. Relax." He leafed through it carefully, page by page. "No doubt about it, Angie. It's a cheat book. Nice size, too. Fits right in the curve of a palm. Don't look so horrified, Angie. I know you didn't do it. My guess is whoever sits next to you in European history had it, got panicky about being caught, and dumped it in the nearest opening, which happened to be your handbag."

"No," said Angie. "Because the person next to me is Nancy Goldstein, and she wouldn't need a book like this. She's a brilliant student. I'm the one who might need it." She heard her own words, shivered, and looked back at Marc again.

Patiently he repeated, "I know you wouldn't do that, Angie. Calm down." And then he ruined it by saying, "But how *did* you get such terrific grades, anyhow?"

Angie glared at him.

"Sorry, sorry," he said quickly.

"Any idiot can do well in typing and sewing, Marc. And English this year is literature I enjoy and understand, so I'm getting a B there. That leaves only one hard course. European history. And that teacher is really into memory work.

Just like this little book. I memorize great. Sometimes I fail when there are essays because I can't analyze things very well, or draw the right conclusions. But I can rattle off a hundred dates and not forget them." Angie was a realist. She giggled and added, "At least, not until the exam is over."

Marc smiled at her absently. He knew Nancy Goldstein fairly well. She wouldn't cheat because she wouldn't need to and because she was honorable. He said, "Who else is taking European history?"

"Everybody I know, Marc. I bet there are at least ten sections of it."

Marc got up from his seat, crossed the restaurant, and dropped the cheat book in the wastebasket under the hostess' desk. When he returned to the table, they talked of other things. Angie seemed to have stopped thinking about the book when it vanished from sight into the wastebasket. But Marc's thoughts kept returning to that neat — oh, so neat, so obvious — little notebook. When he dropped her off at home very late that night, Marc said carefully, "Angie, maybe that cheat book getting into your purse was an accident. The person who made it got into a panic. But it could be something else. Somebody might be trying to frame you."

Angie burst out laughing. "Frame me, Marc? I don't have any enemies. You watch too much television. If they didn't have bad guys, they wouldn't have any action. But real life isn't like that."

She kissed him. Nothing in her life was as satisfying as kissing Marc. And it was very satisfying, too, the way Marc abandoned any other line of thought in order to kiss her back. For several minutes neither was aware of anything except the touch and pressure of each other's love. Marc ran his fingers through Angie's hair and held her in a crushing embrace.

"Not everyone is kind, Angie," he said slowly. "Not everyone is like you and your family. Watch your step. That little book was . . . very calculating. I want you to be careful."

Angie had no idea what he was talking about. She blinked the thought away like a fallen eyelash and kissed him on the nose. Then she kissed each eyebrow and each eyelid. She ran a finger lightly around the hairline of his handsome, dark face and kissed him on the lips once more. "Drive home carefully," she said. "I love you. No fair having an accident."

Marc could not let go of her. There were nights when good-byes were infinitely more difficult than others. Given the chance, Angie might well have driven back to the campus with him, booted his roommates out, and spent the night. It's just as well I have school, she thought. It gives me something I have to do. I can't break down and spend the night with Marc.

"Angie, don't go in," Marc said. "Let's —"

"No. We can't."

"Why can't we? I love you."

"We're waiting," Angie told him. "I have enough to deal with. I'm not adding sex to the list."

"But sex would be fun. Completely fun. No problems involved. I promise."

Angie looked skeptical. "Uh huh. You know, of course, that yours is a minority opinion. Everybody else in the world says that sex brings problems."

"What do they know? Let's do our own research. Please?" His hands drew her closer. She didn't resist.

It would be fun, Angie thought. I do love him.

She said, "No." She gave Marc one more kiss, a solid, quickly terminated kiss that said a goodbye more effectively than words. Then she got out of the car promptly. Sighing, Marc got out his side and caught up to her, walking to the front steps, and kissing her one last time in the doorway.

Angie went in the house quickly, closing the door gently and standing in the soft dark as Marc turned the car engine back on, flooded the yard briefly with light, and then drove off.

It hurt her to have him go. Was I right? she thought. Who *is* right? How do you ever know what's the right thing with a boy you love?

She thought briefly of the strange little book with all its dates and facts.

History was a snap compared to love.

Mary Ellen Kirkwood was alone.

Emotionally and physically alone.

It was a new experience. In all her world, she could not think of one person to whom she could turn. Tell this awful thing to. Get comfort in return.

There was the squad. But looking back, she could see indications that the rest of the squad had heard these rumors and had pulled back from her. *Had doubted. Had wondered.*

Patrick. Patrick would never believe lies about her. Patrick would love her against all odds. She thought of getting up and calling him. But she knew she couldn't. How could she turn to him when she was in trouble and push him away the rest of the time? She ached for his arms around her, comforting her, telling her she was everything he wanted in this world. She wanted his lips kissing her, whispering that he loved her, and would forever.

Mary Ellen was blinded by tears of pain. The people she worked with every day — cheering, laughing, kicking, lifting — they were not sure whether Mary Ellen would steal or not.

The night passed slowly, with Mary Ellen in a private agony she had not known she could suffer. In the morning, barely functioning, she dressed silently. At first she found herself wearing old clothes: dark, retiring, ordinary clothes that another time she might have put on to do housework.

Hiding, she thought. Look at me. Dressing to be anonymous.

It was a game Mary Ellen would not play. Whoever was trying to hurt her would have to play the game alone.

She took a lovely wool skirt from her closet.

It was old, but timeless in style. A bright teal blue pullover matched her eyes and set off her hair. The gold necklace hung like a burnished strand of joy below her throat. She fixed her hair in its most dashing style, weaving ribbons in it. She hung the new dangling earrings from the tiny pierced holes and added more blush than usual. The mirror reflected a young woman who was ready for anything.

I *am* ready for anything, Mary Ellen told herself firmly.

She got to school. She walked down the corridors with her head up. Even when she saw Mrs. Oetjen in the hall, knowing the principal had voiced suspicion to Ardith in the first place, Mary Ellen said nothing but a pleasant good morning.

The first class.

She entered the room tentatively. Troy, with whom she always sat, was not there yet. Mary Ellen walked firmly to her usual seat in the second row, and nobody sat next to her because it was Troy's claim, although they did not have assigned seats here.

Troy arrived late. Mary Ellen's eyes flickered to the door and her heart uttered a prayer.

But Troy's eyes wandered about the room with a casual air. He slid into a seat in the back of the room.

Mary Ellen's stomach knotted painfully. She struggled not to let the knots show in her face, but she knew her cheeks had turned red. Her eyes burned. She turned her face to look down at the desk top. Graffiti long cut and inked in stared back at her. The seat next to her remained empty.

The class monitored Troy's decision. Even the teacher's voice paused midsentence, drawing conclusions.

Mary Ellen sat through a lecture she could not care about, and took notes on a subject she could not concentrate on. She felt as if the world could read her thoughts through that empty chair.

After class she got up fast, telling herself she could catch up to Troy. He hadn't wanted to interrupt class to walk to the front, that was all. He was waiting for her. He —

But he was gone. Swiftly, without lingering, he had left for the next class.

Mary Ellen Kirkwood stood very still. The rest of the class spilled and divided around her like a river around a boulder in its path. She felt as cold as the water in winter.

It was over. Troy was out of her life. He had heard about the shoplifting, and he believed it.

She knew she wouldn't miss the *boy* Troy Frederick, but she would miss what he stood for. He was really boring. He wasn't Patrick, who at this moment she yearned for. He wasn't Pres, who for all his surface coolness was really fun to be with.

Mary Ellen's chin rose fractionally. She walked alone to her second class. It wasn't the end of the world. If Troy thought she was a thief, she didn't need him anyway, not for *any* reason.

CHAPTER

8

European history.

Angie's section.

The major test they had all been dreading.

Mr. Schaefer said, "It's been brought to my attention by the superintendent of schools that there is a resurgence of cheating in my classes. I had not noticed it, I must admit. Maybe I'm getting naive in my old age. I thought this was a better class than most. It saddens me to have to do this, but I am changing the rules for this test."

He's looking at *me!* Angie thought. Her heart failed. A shudder impossible to repress convulsed her slender body.

"Everyone must sit one seat apart," Mr. Schaefer said reluctantly. "All bags and purses and bookbags must be under the seat, with no paper edges showing. I will be walking the aisles during the exam. Does anybody have any questions about the rules?"

Angie felt herself turning colors. I have to stop

119

flushing, she thought, horrified. Somebody will think I really *do* cheat!

She tucked her bag perfectly beneath her chair, snapping the flap tightly so nothing could be slid into it.

Framing me? she thought.

Sick nausea rose in her throat. Every date, every war, every treaty she had ever heard of or memorized vanished from her mind as if she had never studied a minute in her life.

Mr. Schaefer did travel up and down the aisles. But he spent more time standing between Nancy Goldstein and Angie Poletti than anywhere else. Angie knew he expected her to be copying Nancy's paper. And she was so upset, so appalled, so hurt that she could not answer any questions.

It really would look as if she had cheated in the past. Because in the past she had done well, and today she would fail. A sob rose in Angie's throat and she choked on it. Mr. Schaefer looked at her strangely.

She stared at the fill-in blanks on the second page.

She could not think of the answer to one of them.

Not one.

Pres Tilford never studied. Studying was boring. His parents wanted him to study even more than they wanted him to work at Tarenton Fabricators. But he had cheerleading to throw in their faces now. They rarely argued with him about school work. He was lousy on dates and he'd do poorly on this European history exam, but still he'd manage to get a C for the marking period, so who cared?

He wondered briefly about Schaefer being so careful during this test. It was not typical. Schaefer was a pretty relaxed guy. Pres supposed that Dr. Barlow, the superintendent, had come down hard on Schaefer. Threatened him with something. Otherwise Schaefer would never have stood up for forty-seven minutes in a row. Pres hadn't heard much about cheating at Tarenton. Probably some kids would rather cheat than study. Pres couldn't be bothered with either.

He turned in a test that he figured would be about a 78. Pres was good at guessing his grades. It was the only part of academic life he enjoyed — guessing his points and scores.

After class Vanessa walked with him through the corridor. He wasn't thrilled to have her company, but he didn't feel up to getting rid of her, either. Like her or dislike her, Vanessa took up energy. Pres felt low on energy.

"What was that all about?" Vanessa said.

"History of Europe, as far as I could tell."

"Don't be cute. It was about Angie. She's the one who's been cheating. Nobody could figure out how she made honor roll. Well, they'll know now. Did you watch her during the test? She was almost crying out loud."

Pres stopped walking. "You love it, don't you?" he said through his teeth. "You're all hot and excited because you could say that." He knew Angie wouldn't cheat. As one who was pretty willing to bend rules, Pres generally knew the kids who never would. Angie was one of those.

Vanessa tossed her hair. Pres flung it back at her.

Vanessa met his eyes. He had never been able to stare Vanessa down. The girl had abnormal tear ducts. She could stare for hours after everybody else had blinked. She said in a sultry voice, as if they were discussing sex, "I don't think people should be allowed to get away with things just because they're cheerleaders."

Pres tried to see through her, to figure out where she was going with this conversation, but it was like trying to pierce the layers of an onion with his bare eyes. "Don't push, Vanessa," he said softly. "Just remember that I'm a cheerleader, too."

"Mmmmm," Vanessa said, drawing a silken strand of black hair over her lip. "And do you cheat as well?"

His hand came up to hit her.

He actually had to catch his own wrist to stop himself. Breathing hard, wanting to knock her backward against the wall, he managed to control himself and walk away. Very mature, Pres told himself. You're definitely growing up, man — that was admirable the way you didn't kill Vanessa.

He had study hall the next period.

Under the best of circumstances Pres loathed study hall. He could not sit still anywhere. But to be confined to a single chair in a single room, and ordered to crack the books? Forget it.

Pres was almost shaking with anger. He felt like hitting something. Preferably *someone*. He decided to cut study hall. He never studied anyhow, and mad as he was he'd never be able to even pretend to.

Pres circled the halls twice. He didn't have a hall pass. If he got caught and was turned over to Mrs. Oetjen, he'd get detention. Mrs. O. had already warned him once. And if he got detention, he'd miss the next cheerleading practice, and then he'd be in trouble with the squad and Ardith, too. So he had to find somewhere to sit where he wouldn't be noticed.

Pres went up a flight of stairs and circled the floor. Then he sat on a window ledge, looking out at the sparkling lake of Narrow Brook. A door or two beyond him came the distinctive sound of sobbing.

Pres Tilford was no knight in shining armor. He wasn't given to being the kind older brother type, either. Under normal circumstances if he heard weeping, he'd quickly walk the other way. People should solve their problems decently in private, and not throw tears around a public school.

But Kerry was too much with him. Kerry who was gentle and kind; Kerry who was such an astonishing contrast to Vanessa. If it were Kerry weeping, he would go to her at once. He knew it wasn't Kerry, but something in Pres drew him to the sound anyhow.

He slid off the ledge and crossed the hall to an empty classroom. There, huddled against the

123

wall, getting chalk dust on her sweater, was Angie Poletti. "Angie?" he said in amazement. He went right up to her, for the first time in his life taking a girl in his arms for comfort instead of kisses. Angie accepted him with uncontrolled weeping. Wrapping her arms around his chest, she cried and cried.

Pres could not imagine what would upset Angie like that. Unless Marc had dumped her. But he could not imagine Marc dumping her. The rumor Vanessa had told him came back into his mind, but he dismissed it. Angie would never cheat. "What's wrong?" he asked.

"Oh, Pres! I went into the bathroom to fix my hair. You know how there's a double door? So that even when the outer door is open nobody in the hall can see into the girls' room? Well, I was in that tiny hallway about to push the second door open and the girls inside were talking about *me*. They were saying that *I'm* the reason we had special rules during that European history test. They were saying that I've been cheating all year to get my grades. Oh, Pres, it's not true! I can't bear it that people are talking about me like that."

"Nobody would believe that, Angie," he said, rocking her.

"Oh, Pres, didn't you listen to me? *Everybody* believes it!" Angie sniffled and pulled a Kleenex out of her huge purse. The purse had always annoyed Pres. It took up as much space as a suitcase. "They were giggling in this awful sneering way, Pres — *So that's what those goody-goody cheerleaders are really like.*"

124

He could not comfort her. There was nothing she would take from him. I ought to get hold of Marc, Pres thought. If my girl were this upset, I'd want to know about it. "Nobody we care about will believe this," he told her.

Angie looked at him with the first cynicism he had ever seen on her angelic face. "Yes, they will," she said. "Rumors are very strong. They sweep everyone up . . . like a great tide."

He thought of Vanessa, out there busily spreading the rumor even now. He had no idea how to stop her *or* the rumor. People like Vanessa loved gossip, loved spreading it, loved laughing over it.

"Besides," Angie said in total misery, "I got so upset in class that I did rotten on the test. I mean, I got *nothing*. People really *will* think I've been cheating, because I'll get an F on that exam."

Even to Pres it sounded hopeless. He held her tighter, as if he could hug away her problems, and stroked her hair.

Vanessa Barlow had more in common with Pres Tilford than either of them knew. She, too, could not sit still. She, too, found study halls the worst part of school. But she had an advantage over Pres Tilford. He might be the richest boy in school, but her father was the superintendent. She had the connections. She had a permanent hall pass for the year. She was using it now.

She and the Eismar twins were wandering the halls. Actually Vanessa felt like going shopping. There were a number of little specialty shops that ringed the lake at this end, not two blocks from the high school, and she loved going into them. But the twins refused. They weren't used to cutting, not even study hall, and they were afraid of getting into trouble. In vain Vanessa told them they were less likely to get caught *out* of the high school than *in* it.

"Let's find an empty classroom," said Cathleen Eismar. "Then we can sit and talk. I am absolutely *dying* to know why you think it was Angie cheating. I mean, *Angie!* It blows me away to think of *Angie* cheating."

Whatever a conscience might be, Vanessa Barlow lacked one. Not once in her life had Vanessa felt guilt or shame.

She began rumors about Mary Ellen because she was on the squad and Vanessa wasn't. It was so easy. Mary Ellen practically begged for it anyway. Miss Cheerleader. Miss Beauty Contest. Miss Success. Miss Varsity Squad Captain.

Losing out on Varsity was an insult to Vanessa, but anyone could see the cards had been stacked unfairly against her from the beginning. Ardith Engborg didn't like her. Angie and Mary Ellen and Nancy — that whole crowd — they'd seen to it Vanessa wouldn't make it.

But *Pres?* Going out with Mary Ellen when she, Vanessa, was right there? It hurt so much, Vanessa could not bear to think about it.

And then the fun began.

Mary Ellen actually set herself up, buying that jewelry and then refusing to tell people how she could afford it.

Vanessa loved commenting on that jewelry.

Frowning ever so lightly. Dropping the tiniest remark about how peculiar that poor Mary Ellen could be wearing perfume so expensive that even Pres Tilford's mother would think twice before buying it. "Funny," Vanessa would say. "You don't buy that perfume. You invest in it. Megabucks. And Mary Ellen's wearing it. You don't suppose she would — no. *No.* She wouldn't do that, would she? Or what do you think?"

Stealing.

The whispers ran around Tarenton High like rustling leaves.

Shoplifting.

What Vanessa loved best was when the rumors circulated all the way back to her. Softly, stealthily. She would pretend shock and dismay, as if she had never heard anything so awful, so sad.

So many people would be hurt in this Mary Ellen thing! Sometimes Vanessa got a quiver of pleasure just listing them to herself. The little sister Gemma and the parents who thought Mary Ellen was so perfect. The teachers and athletic coaches who were so proud of Mary Ellen. The boys who had crushes on her and the younger girls who admired her as a superwoman.

The cast of characters would change now.

Police departments would question Mary Ellen.

When you thought about it, there was a lot of mileage in this game Vanessa was playing.

Yet no sooner had she begun playing it than everything had changed. Pres dropped Mary Ellen, and even then he didn't return to Vanessa. He fell in love with Angie Poletti.

Everyone could see it. The way he trailed after Angie, putting up with her little brother and that chunky girl friend of his. Eyes like a puppy, always on Angie.

Angie was so thoroughly Marc's that you couldn't believe Pres was even considering Angie. And yet it was like Pres, when you analyzed it. Pres wanted to have it all. The very fact that he couldn't have Angie made her that much more desirable.

Angie. A true goody-goody. Lovey-dovey and sweet. Deep down, Angie must harbor the same rage and frustration that Vanessa did, but Angie had control. In all the years they'd been in school together, Vanessa had never seen Angie be anything but an angel.

And Angie had been made Homecoming Queen, when Vanessa had wanted it almost more than she had ever wanted anything in her life.

Angie. The dear, good, and thoughtful sweetheart of Tarenton High. Vanessa was determined to fix her . . . get her . . . in some way.

The only solution Vanessa could see was to make Angie less dear, less good, and less sweet.

So she came up with a plan. It wasn't as much fun as with Mary Ellen, because the teachers had a hard time catching on and because Shelley and Cathleen Eismar couldn't be persuaded to help spread that rumor. They had as much faith in Angie as Pres did.

But it had worked today. Right there in European history it worked. So she had to go through

128

her father to accomplish it. What else were fathers for?

Vanessa reached the top of the stairs they were climbing before Shelley and Cathleen. What good shape she was in. No cheerleader could have a better physique. I should be on the squad, Vanessa thought darkly. For the thousandth time her anger boiled up. Behind her Cathleen and Shelley were out of breath. Vanessa felt contempt for them, as they sucked air into starved lungs. Silently the three girls walked past the open door of an empty classroom.

Empty, that is, except for Pres Tilford and Angie Poletti.

Vanessa, Shelley, and Cathleen saw them like a cameo. Framed by the door, caught against the dark, flat background of the chalkboard.

Pres was kissing Angie's upturned lips. He was smoothing away tears on the ivory cheeks, running his hands over her gleaming hair.

The twins gasped audibly.

Vanessa slipped out of sight before Pres and Angie could look up. There was a moment of silence. Then Angie said awkwardly, "Oh. Hi."

In unison the twins said, "Hi," the syllable lasting a long time. Their little gossiping minds drew little gossiping conclusions.

Laughter instead of jealousy filled Vanessa.

Truly, Angie and Mary Ellen had more in common than they knew.

How well — how generously — they had set themselves up!

CHAPTER

Mary Ellen looked at her wallet.

Money was the only thing you could count on. People abandoned you, friends betrayed you, but money would always buy you something.

Mary Ellen didn't have enough to buy the purse she had her eye on. Why did she always fall in love with Marnie's things? She never wanted a purse from the discount store or shoes from the cut-rate chain. She always wanted the top of the line.

But looking could be almost as much fun as buying. Especially when you knew you would be able to buy eventually. And God knew, if nobody else did, that Mary Ellen needed something to cheer herself up.

She slipped her wallet back into the old purse that would have to last another three weeks. The new purse would match her winter coat. She had an uncomfortable feeling that the coat had once belonged to Mrs. Tilford and ended up in the Thrift Shop run by hospital volunteers. But Pres had never mentioned it, possibly because he never looked at his mother long enough to notice her clothes. Anyway, it was a lovely coat and Mary Ellen looked beautiful in it.

Mary Ellen took the bus to the shopping center. Looking out the window she noticed Patrick Henley on his garbage truck. A line from some old movie, or old book, came into her mind. *Honey, I been rich and I been poor, and believe me, rich is better.*

Oddly enough Patrick was earning a lot of money, and hard worker that he was, would earn more and more. But Mary Ellen didn't just want money; she wanted status. I'm sorry, Patrick, she thought, her head turning to watch his truck in spite of herself. You won't do. Much as I may want you, actually yearn for you, you won't do.

She got off the bus thinking of the handbag in Marnie's. It was a soft, dark leather, so supple it was like stroking velvet. Its shoulder strap had intricate knots at the lower end and inside the purse were two zippered dividers and a lovely slim wallet that reeked of gold credit cards and expense accounts.

"Why, hi, Mary Ellen."

She jumped out of her fantasies and saw the Eismar twins beside her. "Hi, Cathy. Hi, Shelley. How are you?"

Mercifully they did not snub her like the last time. She could not imagine why. They must have heard those rumors back then. Why dismiss them now?

"Want to go into the Farm Shop to have ice cream with us?" invited Cathleen.

Had she made everything up? Did she have an active imagination? Was this horrid rumor confined to Mrs. Oetjen and Mrs. Engborg? Did Shelley and Cathy like her after all?

"I'd love to," Mary Ellen said warily.

The girls giggled and chatted like old pals. Shelley wanted to talk about the basketball game coming up and Cathleen wanted to talk about the rumor that Pres was now going out with Angie.

"Oh, no," said Mary Ellen. "They're not dating. Angie is all but engaged to Marc. You know that."

"But Pres is with Angie all the time now," said Cathleen.

"Just because of cheerleading," said Mary Ellen. "She's lonely with Marc off at college and Pres takes her around now and then."

The twins snorted. "Lonely! You better believe she's not lonely anymore, Mary Ellen. Nobody could be lonely with Pres kissing her." They told her in detail what they had seen in the empty classroom at school.

Mary Ellen could hardly take it in. She knew Pres would do anything, given an inch — but *Angie?* Angie the angel was two-timing Marc the magnificent?

"And you know what was funny?" Shelley Eismar said.

"What?" Mary Ellen said. Nothing was funny that she could see.

"Vanessa Barlow was so thrilled to think that Marc was available after all that she called him up to ask if he'd take her to the basketball game Saturday and go to Susan Yardley's party afterwards. And you know what else?"

"I can guess," Mary Ellen said dryly. "He didn't know about Angie and Pres till Vanessa told him, did he?"

Vanessa was disgusting. Give her one corner of a rumor and she spread the whole sheet. Thank heaven Vanessa had not made Varsity. Then life would really be rotten. Vanessa every day. It was enough to make a person shudder.

If Vanessa's heard this shoplifting rumor, Mary Ellen thought, I'm sunk. She'll tell the entire universe. "Nice talking to you," she said to the twins, although it hadn't been. "I'm going to poke around Marnie's for a while."

Slyly, Cathleen said, "You like that store, don't you?"

The voice left no room for doubt. Cathleen knew the rumor. Cathleen was pouring acid, not friendliness. Mary Ellen's heart sank, but her chin rose. "I certainly do," she said, staring at Cathleen, daring her to say more.

But Cathleen didn't dare. Mary Ellen left some quarters on the counter and walked out.

Who could you trust in this world? Not even Angie?

Oh, Pres, she thought. The old yearning for Pres's money and style and company overwhelmed her again. Date me, Pres. I'd look so lovely on your arm. I'd go everywhere with you, do everything with you.

But it was an empty dream.

And if Troy couldn't be bothered with her, neither could Pres. The boys were depressingly alike. But as always, Mary Ellen felt better just walking into Marnie's.

The lovely displays. A carefully draped velvet cloth showing off a delicate necklace and an unusual scarf, with a pair of wonderful earrings beside them. She paused to finger the imported sweaters: soft, beautiful hues this year, muted and infinitely sophisticated. On the other side of the sweaters: soft, beautiful hues this year, muted and single tray held a dozen lovely rings on a bed of plum velvet.

No matter how much laundry she did, she would never be able to buy one of those rings. She would have to wait to be a successful model in New York to wear something like that.

It was a filigree of gold with a delicate flower of translucent precious stone set in it.

Mary Ellen could not resist it. She slipped it over one of her long, slim fingers. It was a lovely hand. Not a broken fingernail, not a chipped spot of polish. She squinted to see her hand against the plum fabric and it looked like a photograph in *Vogue*, the flawless gem on the flawless skin.

Sighing, she slipped the ring back on the tray, and left Marnie's almost at a run.

She was, after all, nothing but a poor, small-town cheerleader — dumped by two boyfriends in succession, the center of rumors she could not bear to think of.

The city bus arrived almost immediately so at least she didn't have to stand in the cold contemplating her miserable state. When Mary Ellen got home, the car was available. Rather than chat with the family who expected cheery little stories all through dinner, Mary Ellen decided to do her laundry immediately instead of after dinner. She literally threw the bags of dirty clothes and the detergent into the old station wagon. Driving out she took a corner fast enough to leave a patch of rubber. It certainly did not make her feel better. What did Pres find so wonderful about speeding? Mary Ellen just felt more nervous than ever, afraid she'd have an accident or get a ticket.

The simple repetitive tasks of laundry calmed her the way even window-shopping at Marnie's could not. Mary Ellen sat for a time, watching the laundry swish in the soapsuds behind the round glass door of the biggest machine. She folded. She perspired from the heat of the dryers and folded some more. Reaching into her old vinyl purse she felt around for a Kleenex to mop the perspiration from her face.

And there, lying in the bottom of her purse, glittering up at her, lay the magnificent flowered ring from Marnie's.

Angie was sitting in the front seat of Marc's car. She had never sat next to him like this without his hands touching her, never sat next to him without his fingers in her hair, on her cheeks.

135

Now when she twined her fingers in his, his hands lay stiff, unresponsive, rejecting.

Angie thought her world had crumbled. She was not used to this kind of problem. Financial problems, school work problems, problems with the weather, or her complexion, yes. But never had Angie Poletti had problems with the boy she loved.

"Please, Marc," she said desperately. "Please. Pres was just being comforting. You have to believe me."

"I believe you."

"No, you don't. I can tell by the way you're staring out the window instead of at me. You don't believe a word of my side of the story."

"Yes, I do. It's just that —"

His voice stopped. Angie nodded tearfully. "It's just that where there's smoke, there's fire, huh? Well, I know what you mean. I felt that way when I heard the rumors about Mary Ellen shoplifting."

Marc was so astounded he turned sharply in the seat and looked at her for the first time all evening. *"Mary Ellen shoplifting?"*

"So the rumors run. I don't believe it. On the other hand, how can someone as hard up for money as Mary Ellen be wearing jewelry from Marnie's?"

Angie ached with the ugliness of the world. How could so many things go wrong during what should be their happiest year? The wonderful cheerleading squad, torn and shredded by ugly rumors.

"It's very strange," Marc said.

"What is?"

"There are only six cheerleaders on Varsity. I've heard rumors about three of you. Angie, Pres, and Mary Ellen. Fifty percent of you, the objects of vicious rumors. Very, very strange."

Angie shrugged.

"Don't shrug," Marc said. "It needs more than a shrug. There's something very wrong."

"Maybe we're not a very nice squad," Angie said, and now her tears came in earnest, flooding her thoughts, drenching her face.

Marc held her at last, and Angie was so relieved she didn't notice that his hug did not contain affection, but thoughtfulness. "It's a very nice squad," said Marc. "But somebody doesn't like you very much. Think, Angie. Half the squad is getting knifed. Who would do that?"

Angie thought, but came up with nobody.

"Come on, honor roll scholar," he said teasingly, lovingly. *"Think."*

No sarcasm in his voice. No accusation. Just affection now . . . and urgency. Marc said, "I have a feeling this is an avalanche, Angie. It's swelling. It's getting worse. It has to be stopped before someone is very badly hurt."

"I knew you would call," Kerry said.

Pres settled into the pillows on his bed and lay back, telephone cradled under his chin, a smile on his face. What a nice voice Kerry had. Warm, friendly, *nice.* "How did you know?" he said.

"I couldn't read all your eyebrow signals last

night," said Kerry, "so I knew you would telephone me to explain them."

Pres explained some of his eyebrow signals. Kerry giggled breathlessly into her end of the phone. They flirted by wire. Kerry had no experience at this and Pres had a lot. But this was the first time Pres had really cared about the girl he was calling. It added a great deal to the conversation.

Kerry said at last, "It was awful when Andrew took me home."

"What was awful about it?"

"He could tell I liked you. He asked me about it. He said he wanted to know what was between us."

"What did you say?" Pres was amazed at the tension he was feeling. He, Pres Tilford, lady killer, was sick with worry that Kerry would not give up Andrew.

"I said you and I were going out this weekend." Kerry shivered. Andrew had simply nodded and accepted it. No arguing, no bad-mouthing Pres. But she did not think it was because Andrew wasn't hurt. He just had a lot of self-control. Having your girl friend walk when you were in the midst of the triumph of your life must be awful.

I'm awful, Kerry thought. Only awful people do things like that.

Pres talked to her about their date to come.

What's happening to me? Kerry thought. Am I growing selfish and mean? Or is this real love?

* * *

Mary Ellen's self-control was gone.

The sight of the ring at the bottom of her purse tore her heart loose from her chest. She wept uncontrollably.

Mary Ellen went on with the laundry, feeling as if it were a task in hell. Tears rolled off her cheeks and dampened the sheets all over again.

Had she really stolen the ring?

Was she really a shoplifter?

Maybe she *wasn't* paying for this stuff she acquired. Maybe she just *thought* she was. Maybe there were no rumors. Only truth.

Mary Ellen Kirkwood steals.

The ring. Right there in her purse.

Mary Ellen burned her fingers on a metal snap straight from the hottest dryer. Sucking the finger, she thought, *No.* I have the sales slips from the purchases I made. I *know* I didn't shoplift.

Could she have forgotten to put this ring back, though?

Left it on her finger?

Let it drop accidentally into her bag?

Or had she wanted it so much she actually had stolen it?

Mary Ellen finished folding. Carefully she divided everything into piles for each customer. She had a sense that if she was just orderly, the universe would return to its fixed position, all this — and most of all the ring — would go away.

And then it hit her. Like a sharp knife, stabbing.

How was she going to return the ring?

She couldn't call the store up. "Oh, listen. I accidentally stole an expensive precious ring from you. Mind if I drop it off?"

Drop it off. She could drop it down a storm drain. She could drop it into the last remaining cup of detergent at the bottom of the huge box, and drop the box into the huge trash basket under the folding table, and nobody would ever find a thing. Proof would vanish.

And then, Mary Ellen thought, the tears hotter than any dryer, scalding her soul as well as her eyes, then I really would be a thief.

The woman with the rotting teeth waved goodbye and left the laundromat. The tired young mother staggered out with so much laundry that she must have quadruplets. In came a shifty man with torn work pants. He tossed the contents of a small plastic bag into a small washing machine and dropped quarters into the vending machine for detergent. A couple eating jelly doughnuts walked in, arguing fiercely about whether they had enough laundry to warrant using the larger, more expensive machines.

Mary Ellen looked into her purse again. Maybe the ring was an optical illusion. A mirage.

But no.

The ring glittered cruelly. Its sparkles mocked her.

There was no way out. No hope. She had no friends anymore because of the rumors. Her fellow cheerleaders had heard the rumors. They had not abandoned her — but they hadn't gathered around, either. As for Troy, he had dumped her.

Mrs. Engborg and Mrs. Oetjen didn't believe in her. She could not possibly confide in her parents. They would dissolve in shock.

Mary Ellen seriously considered running away from home.

But to run away, she needed a place to go. Right now she had barely enough money to get to Wickfield, let alone New York City.

There was nothing to do but carry the laundry back to the car, go home to do her studying, and wait for the ax to fall where it might. She hoisted the first basket. It was almost unbearably heavy.

But I have to bear it, she thought. Whatever comes, I will have to bear it. She took one basket out to the car.

The tears began again. She pushed the door to re-enter the laundromat and the door felt ten feet tall and made of lead. Mary Ellen leaned on it in despair, and nothing happened.

"Let me get it," said a man.

She stepped aside gratefully, brushing furtively at the tear streaks on her face. "Thank you," she whispered.

"You're welcome." A gentle voice. Very masculine. Very deep. Her heart almost stopped. She looked up.

It was Patrick.

Oh, I can't deal with anything more! Don't make me face somebody I know. Please God let me vanish from the face of the earth.

"You've been crying," he said.

They stared at each other. The shifty guy had his washing machine started and wanted to leave,

141

but they were blocking the door. Patrick held the door for him, his eyes never leaving Mary Ellen. She had never yet stood close to Patrick Henley without being overwhelmed by him. That dark wave of hair, those wide cheeks, those deep, sexy eyes.

At last she said, "I've had a hard day."

"I guess so." He escorted her into the laundromat. The only thing worse than meeting a boy in this nasty, dirty, low-class place would be going to prison for stealing jewelry, she thought. "Mary Ellen," he said, "this is enough laundry for an army. What have you Kirkwoods been up to? Only garbage men get this dirty."

She began weeping again.

"Don't cry," he said. "What's wrong? Tell me."

She could not speak.

He carried the last basket for her. They sat in her mother's decrepit station wagon, his arms around her, her head on his chest. Life was so terrible. And yet, in this position, being comforted by this boy, Mary Ellen wanted life to be even *more* terrible, so that she could stay forever in the safety of Patrick's embrace.

"Tell me," he repeated, and she did.

The story was easier to tell than she had expected. When she was not able to utter the dreadful words, he supplied them for her. "Oh, Pat," she said finally, almost drowning in her tears, "I don't know what to do!"

You didn't deal in the most basic problem of civilized life — getting rid of waste and trash — without learning to be practical. Patrick said,

142

"First of all, you can't have evidence like that in your purse. If you get caught with that ring there, you're in deep and serious trouble. So what we'll do is, we'll get it back to Marnie's right away."

"Patrick, how can we do that?" she cried desperately. "I can't walk in there and tell them it materialized in my handbag like a miracle from heaven."

"No. Of course not. But I can. I pick up the trash at that shopping center, Mary Ellen. I'll go into Marnie's and say I found the ring on the pavement out by their trash cans."

"They won't believe it," she said instantly.

"They'll have to believe it. I'll be bringing it back, won't I? They won't have any other explanation, will they?" Patrick delved into her purse. She thought he would take the ring, but instead he handed her her hairbrush. "You look awful," he told her. "I never thought I'd see the day, but this is it. Fix your hair."

Her breath was still jagged. "I don't care about my hair."

"I do. I love you. I love your hair, too."

"I don't want to be loved for my hair," she said morosely.

"Wow. If you don't want to be loved for your hair, how come you spend a jillion hours fixing it in all those fancy ways and twists?" said Patrick.

She looked up at him ruefully. He was on the mark, all right. His eyes crinkled a little at the corners, a laugh starting. She could not help herself, and began laughing, too. The laughter changed to loving, and he kissed the tear stains

143

on her cheeks and she kissed his lips, which were salty with her own tears. "Oh, Patrick," she said at last, "I don't know how to thank you."

Patrick took the ring from her purse, slipped it into his pocket, and said, "You do know how to thank me. The question is, will you do it?"

He was saving her life. He was returning the ring for her. Rescuing her as surely as if she had been drowning in the ocean. She knew what he was asking. *Go out with me. Date me. Love me.*

The attraction she felt for Patrick was stronger than ever. But just as much as ever, Mary Ellen was horrified at appearing in public with a garbage man.

He's my knight in shining armor, she thought. And if his gallant steed happens to be a garbage truck, well, that's how it is in Tarenton. Hot spot of high romance that it is.

Very lightly, she kissed him.

He kissed her back far more intensely.

He was too much to be dismissed easily. In the parking lot by the light of the laundromat — the last place Mary Ellen had ever wanted to be seen by anybody on earth — they kissed fervently.

"I love you," said Patrick at one point.

She did not answer. She kissed him, but she did not commit herself.

CHAPTER

Olivia and Nancy were sprawled on their backs on the gymnasium floor. They'd had a long day in class and each of them felt it was absolutely impossible even to *think* about cheerleading practice. "When you can't even hoist your eyelids," Nancy said, "you *know* cheerleading is out."

Olivia yawned so hugely her small body arched and slumped back down. The girls talked a little about Michael, Olivia's boyfriend, and then about Alex, Nancy's boyfriend.

Nancy said, "Olivia?"

"Mmmm?"

"This is going to sound silly, but does it ever seem to you that we're not the same squad we used to be? I feel split off from the rest. Everybody's upset about something, but I don't feel a part of it."

Olivia sat up immediately, as if energized by

those depressing words. Leaning forward to look down on Nancy's sleepy face, she said, "I know just what you mean! I haven't said anything, but the last few weeks have been awful. Every time I turn around I'm defending Mary Ellen to somebody who thinks she's a shoplifter, or I'm defending Angie to somebody who thinks she's a cheat, or I'm insisting that Pres is just being nice to Angie, and really Angie is still going out with Marc."

"Rumors are so terrifying," Nancy said. She sat up, too, and absently tugged at her socks, smoothing the ridges. If only life could be smoothed so readily! "After you've heard them a few times, you begin to wonder. Little things come back to you, and you half think it could all be true."

Olivia shuddered. "And I have a mother who believes every word of it and wants me off the squad so I won't associate with any of these low-lifes again."

"How awful. At least my mother shrugs it off. She says you have to endure this kind of thing sometimes, and that you have to be on Angie's and Mary Ellen's team every minute."

Olivia and Nancy had never been particularly close, but these admissions drew them together. "And what about Walt?" Olivia said. "What do you make of him?"

Nancy was thoughtful. "He's a true loner. You get boys like Pres, or Troy — they *pretend* to be loners. They like the *idea* of being loners. But Pres and Troy are party boys. Now Walt. I think he's going to spend his life on the sidelines. Watching. Maybe reporting, like his parents. But not really *in* it, if you know what I mean."

Olivia shuddered. "It sounds sad to me. He'll miss out on a lot."

"Or be hurt by less," Nancy pointed out.

Across the wide gleaming gym floor, Mary Ellen appeared in the doorway of the girls' locker room. Thinner now. Not lithe and lovely, but simply thin. Wan and drawn.

Olivia said, "I would never have believed that Mary Ellen could look so awful."

"Do you think she's sick?"

"Not physically."

"Olivia," Nancy said in a tense, anxious voice. "Olivia, what do you *really* think?"

"I decided I didn't dare think about it too hard," Olivia said.

The girls stared at each other. Reflected pain — the possible destruction of the squad they loved so much — lay in their eyes. If something did not happen soon to bring them all together, one by one the cheerleaders would fall away — torn off from the squad by rumor.

Ardith Engborg jogged slowly out of the coach's office. She was carrying a box of designer Kleenex and even as she ran, she had to stop and pull one out. "I hab this terrible code," she said thickly.

"Oh, you poor thing," Olivia said, immediately moving away. She had been sick enough in her life. She did not expose herself to other people's colds if she could help it.

Nancy moved back with Olivia, but for a different reason. "We need to talk," she said to Olivia. "The six of us. As a squad."

"Talk about what?" Olivia said.

"Don't be dense. About these rumors. We need to sit down and bring all these terrible things out into the open and deal with them."

"What a horrible thought. Who knows what awful things one of us might say — or learn? No. That would just make it worse, Nancy. Leave it alone. All things pass. Eventually the rumors will dry up and disappear."

Nancy glanced over her shoulder at Mary Ellen. The former golden girl walked as if she were carrying the barbells from the weight room, and they were breaking her stamina. "I don't think the rumors will go away by themselves, Olivia."

"Well, if you're really convinced that group therapy is the answer, *you* take charge. I'll join Walt on the sidelines and avoid some of life's pain."

Pres entered the gym cartwheeling. It was one of the things he was very good at, and many of their cheers featured him cartwheeling around. You had to capitalize on your strengths. What a contrast the happy Pres was to quiet Angie and drooping Mary Ellen!

"What on earth are you celebrating, Pres?" Olivia said.

Pres's grin was alternately right side up and upside down as he spun around them. He arrived next to Mary Ellen, grinning, tipped up to meet her eyes — one leg in the air, hand flung apart, frozen like someone in a kindergarten tag game. "Life," he informed them all, "is terrific."

Mary Ellen looked at him with utter disgust and pushed him. He was off balance and fell in a sprawl to the floor. On the way he caught Mary Ellen's ankle and pulled her down on top of himself and kissed her.

Normally Mary Ellen would have rejoiced at his attention. Most of all at his physical attention. Today she extricated herself as if he were a dangerous machine complete with cutting blades. She didn't even speak to him.

The rest of the squad gaped at her. Mary Ellen? Avoiding the kisses of Pres?

Mrs. Engborg sneezed violently, doubling over, and crushing the Kleenex box against her chest.

"That was very graceful," Nancy teased. "Sort of a new gymnastics move. We'll call it the tissue grab."

Nobody laughed. Nobody even smiled.

Olivia and Nancy exchanged glances. What was the matter with them all? Were they going to be stuck in this joyless, unhappy association?

Ardith Engborg sighed.

Nancy thought they were about due for a pep talk. Lack of spirit. Need for enthusiasm. But no. It wasn't a pep talk Ardith gave.

The coach said, "This is no cold. This is the flu. In fact, I think this is some rare Far Eastern flu that only I have gotten this year. It could even be fatal."

Olivia retreated several paces.

149

Walt said, "I recommend two aspirin to prevent death."

Nobody laughed at this, either.

Mary Ellen pulled herself together and said, "Go home and get some rest, Mrs. Engborg. I can lead the practice." She looked and sounded as if the only thing she could lead was a funeral march.

"No," said Ardith. "We're all tired, and that leaves us all vulnerable to sickness. I'm going home, and we're going to cancel practice. You're in good shape, but you're dragging like tired old work horses, which is no way to begin basketball season. Take the day off."

It was unheard of — Ardith Engborg giving them time off.

"And nobody is to come down with my flu," she said severely. "It is forbidden to get sick. Is that clear?"

Walt spoke for them. "Clear, Sergeant."

Ardith blew them a weary kiss and trudged out of the gym.

"I hope you feel better," Nancy called after her. I hope *we* feel better, she thought grimly. We look like derelicts, not cheerleaders. "Let's all go to the Farm Shop at the mall," she said brightly. "I think we need a team meeting. How about a booth in the corner? And chocolate sundaes?"

Walt seconded this. "Great idea. I'm always ready for ice cream. I've got room in my Jeep for three."

"And I'll take whoever's left," Pres said. He

beamed at everybody. He was caught up in some daydream so pleasurable that Nancy doubted if he had registered a single thing that was going on. Who *is* he in love with? she thought.

The Jeep and the Porsche took them all to the shopping mall.

It was a fairly good-sized indoor mall, with two anchor stores and seventeen smaller ones. There were a half dozen miniature boutiques lining the center of the mall, scattered among the fountains, planters of ferns, and redwood benches. Going to the mall was a common source of entertainment. Nobody was surprised to recognize lots of friends.

It was Pres who split first.

He saw Kerry — or rather, he saw her gleaming jacket — vanishing into the department store. For all his euphoria, Pres knew what was happening on the squad; Angie had wept in his arms, after all. But he had a very uneasy feeling about Nancy's desire to talk together. Talks like that at Pres's house invariably ended in screaming and yelling. Pres didn't want to see his fellow cheerleaders angry and shouting, or in pain and cringing. He was too happy. He wanted to think about Kerry, plan for Kerry, talk to Kerry.

And so when he saw her jacket he also saw a way out. He told himself it was only for ice cream, and the squad could socialize without him. "See you later," Pres said, chasing after Kerry.

"But Pres!" Nancy cried. Nancy herself barely knew Kerry and even if she had recognized the jacket would never have guessed that this was the girl Pres was daydreaming about. She simply had no idea where Pres was going or why. Oh, well, Nancy thought. The rest of us can still talk.

They passed an enormous planter with tall, drooping fig trees and feathery, wispy asparagus ferns. Opposite the planter was the Farm Shop. Its huge glass windows gave the patrons in the front row of booths a complete view of the mall. It also gave the shoppers a complete view of them — and there in booth two was Troy and some girl. Lovely, slender, dark — nobody they had ever seen before. Definitely not a Tarenton girl. Troy looked fashionable and mysterious, and she looked beautiful and jet set.

Mary Ellen actually whimpered.

Oh, no! Nancy thought, horrified. Olivia and Nancy and Angie drew together to protect Mary Ellen from Troy's view, but it was very obvious that the only view Troy cared about was this unknown girl. If Mary Ellen had ever meant anything at all to Troy, she didn't now.

Nancy abandoned all hope of an ice cream get-together. She would never even get Mary Ellen in the front door of the Farm Shop, and Mary Ellen and Angie were the two who most needed the talk. Now what? she thought irritably.

Mary Ellen wrenched her eyes away from Troy. She hadn't been in love with him anyhow; she was silly to react so deeply to this. But how easily he had replaced her!

"Olivia!" came a shout.

It was Olivia's boyfriend, Michael. Like the

track star he was, Michael loped across the mall, swept Olivia up in his arms, and almost tossed her in the air. Mary Ellen watched them through a fog. She saw two people suited for each other: their heights and weights meshed as well as their personalities and dreams. Why, oh, why, she thought drearily, couldn't that happen to *me?*

"Thought you had practice!" Michael said. "Why didn't you tell me you were free? Come on. I'm about to go to Hamburg King for a burger."

Hamburg King was on the other side of Tarenton. Olivia said, "Ooooo, terrific." She kissed Michael and waved good-bye to what was left of the squad. Nancy glared at Olivia, but Olivia pretended not to notice. If anything, she hauled Michael away faster than he hauled her.

Mary Ellen, turning slightly to watch them go, found her eyes resting on the display window of Marnie's.

Cold dread shivered up her arms, lifting the tiny blonde hairs and giving her goose bumps. Patrick had taken the ring back. He had called to tell her so. On the telephone, his voice consoled and reassured her as easily as his arms when they sat together.

He's such a good person, Mary Ellen thought. If I can have Patrick, why do I care about Troy? Why do I care about Pres?

But it was not so much the boys themselves right now, as the affection itself — the knowledge that she, Mary Ellen, was special, was worth knowing.

Right now, with these rumors, however, the knowledge might be that Mary Ellen was dangerous, was *not* worth knowing.

I have to go back into Marnie's, Mary Ellen thought. She stared through a group of junior high boys who were being stupid the way only thirteen-year-old boys could be, showing off for the important cheerleaders they recognized. Mary Ellen hardly saw them. Through their skinny arms and legs she saw the window at Marnie's. A new display. Colors that hadn't been there when she —

When the ring —

When —

She had to know. She had to know how that ring got into her purse. By accident or by design. "Let's go into Marnie's," she said to Angie and Nancy. "They've got a whole new shipment of hats. We can try them on. I love to try on hats."

Nancy went white. Angie gasped.

Not only did the girls know about the shoplifting rumor, they knew it supposedly happened in Marnie's.

Mary Ellen swallowed the sick feeling that rose in her throat. She had to go through with this. It was like getting back on the horse that threw you.

All three girls had forgotten Walt.

For all his genial attitude, his unfailing kindness and brotherly affection, Walt maintained his anonymous quality. He kept to himself more than any of them. Perhaps it was safer that way. He would certainly never get hurt as Mary Ellen and

Angie had, leaving their souls open to the world. But it was also a little sad.

Walt said, "I'm not crazy about trying on girls' hats. I've got to get some blank cassettes, though, and the department store is having a sale. I'll go over there and catch up to you girls later, okay?"

Mary Ellen watched him go as if she were watching a film. She had a sense of approaching her own doom, and Walt, his straightforward, straight-shouldered body disappearing down the crowded mall center, seemed to be abandoning her to it.

Angie Poletti decided to shrug it all off.

She had had to endure two horrible rumors herself, and it was better for everybody not to think about the horrible rumor involving Mary Ellen. She liked simple pleasures; she liked trying on hats; and she liked Marnie's. She decided to think no further. Linking arms with Mary Ellen, she said, "Good idea. The first hat I'm going after is that peculiar purple one in the window."

"Purple is really your color, too," Nancy agreed.

"Are you being sarcastic? I think I look like an overcooked lobster when I wear purple."

"Hi, there," said a sultry voice.

All three cheerleaders recognized that voice. Only Vanessa had that husky, threatening quality in her voice.

"Hi," Nancy said without welcome. She was still furious at Vanessa for all the destructive things she'd done to them, including telling her parents about Alex.

"Going into Marnie's?" Vanessa said. "They have the most beautiful hair ornaments in, Mary Ellen. Lovely in your hair. You must ask them to unlock the cabinet."

She certainly heard the rumors, Angie thought. Now she's going to enjoy herself sticking the knife into Mary Ellen and turning it.

Angie glanced at Vanessa and was shocked at Vanessa's expression. The girl's eyes had lit greedily, cruelly, on Mary Ellen.

She *loves* these rumors, Angie thought. She is *really* evil.

Angie pulled Mary Ellen ahead with her, leaving Vanessa back with Nancy. Coming to the mall had been all Nancy's idea anyway; let her handle Vanessa.

Pres Tilford didn't actually run. That would be beneath his dignity. But he moved quickly through the shoppers: the elderly ladies with their bulging black handbags, the mothers pushing strollers, the teenagers staring into shop windows. Through the turnstile and into the store, his eyes never moved from the silvery grey jacket with the distinctive lavender strip that Kerry wore.

He had seen Troy going into the Farm Shop with some girl. Pretty, definitely, but nothing compared to Kerry, who was lovely and soft and nice. I'll round up Kerry, he thought, and we'll join Troy at the Farm Shop.

It occurred to Pres that Troy should have been with Mary Ellen.

Troy dumped her, he thought. Well, it wasn't surprising. Troy couldn't be pinned down easily and he was superficial, but it was too bad. Mary Ellen was not having an easy year, all things told.

He thought briefly of the shoplifting rumors that still swirled around Tarenton High, but Kerry vanished behind light bulbs and Pres had to run past paint brushes and ladders to keep her in sight. He wanted to yell her name, to shout *Kerry!* at the top of his lungs. But she might hate that. He knew *he* would hate that. He preferred keeping his dating life private.

What was Kerry doing in the hardware section, anyway?

Her silvery jacket whisked out of sight behind the last aisle and Pres broke into a run. There was a rear exit to the store and he might lose her.

He burst around the corner, almost skidding on the marble floor, a grin of pleasure already on his face — and it was not Kerry at all. It was some woman about thirty looking at flashlight batteries. Pres stared at her as if she had a disease and she looked back at him as if he were psychotic. "Sorry," Pres said lamely, his cheeks flaring red with embarrassment. He fled back in the other direction, feeling like a true fool.

He slowed his pace, telling himself nobody had seen him. Even if anybody had, nobody would care. Nobody would know what the hurry was. His embarrassment was still private.

That he, Pres Tilford, should act like this! It

was unthinkable. Running like a little kid. Literally panting for Kerry.

What excuse would he give the other cheerleaders? None. He'd look suave and mysterious and pretend it wasn't their business if he took to jogging down malls after strange women in silver ski jackets.

Pres emerged in the large central core of the mall and tried to spot the squad. The place was too big; there were too many people. He could circle for an hour and still not find them.

They should have posted somebody to flag me down, he thought, conveniently forgetting that *he* was the one who had deserted *them*.

At last he saw Angie framed in the window of Marnie's. He would never know why that place was so popular. They had the dumbest garbage he'd ever seen there. Angie was posturing in front of a mirror, wearing a ridiculous purple hat that had a brim on one side but not the other, and a swoop to it that made even Angie look slightly bent in the middle.

Farther into the store's single aisle, Pres could see Mary Ellen bending over a counter, Nancy holding a blouse up to herself and Vanessa —

Oh, God. Vanessa.

Pres had never intended to enter Marnie's anyhow, but now he definitely would not enter. Where was Walt? How was it that Walt managed to stay out of all the difficult aspects of life?

Pres thought of what Vanessa would say if she could have seen him chasing after some matron through the entire discount store.

The store windows angled out in two large bays. Pres leaned to the side of one of them. It gave him a peculiar slanted view of the store.

Angie took off the purple hat with a gasp, as if it housed a wasp's nest, and an expression of horror came over her face.

Pres straightened up and turned to look directly at Angie. She might have been watching a murder. He turned quickly to look where she was looking. A robbery in Hats? A mugging among the Cruise Wear?

He saw nothing. Mary Ellen, Vanessa, Nancy, poking through things. Mary Ellen giving a sigh and walking toward the exit.

I could do my good deed for the day, Pres thought. Take Mary Ellen to the Farm Shop for ice cream. Cheer her up a little.

Angie, sick fear still on her face, followed Mary Ellen. Her fingers stretched out to catch Mary Ellen. But Mary Ellen was striding now, passing Angie, leaving the store. Angie looked at Pres with mute appeal, but Pres didn't know what she wanted.

The terrible rumors came back to him forcefully.

Mary Ellen Kirkwood steals.

Mary Ellen Kirkwood shoplifts.

Pres blocked Mary Ellen's path. He had no idea what to do. To turn her in, to let her go. Undoubtedly, Angie had seen it happen. It was true. Wonderful, beautiful Mary Ellen — a common thief.

159

CHAPTER

11

Angie had to do the right thing.

But this was not simply a matter of what was right and what was wrong. There were a lot of avenues here . . . and grim pitfalls if she made the wrong choice.

So little time to think!

No way to consult her mother, to phone her boyfriend.

Angie thought with desperate speed. She was not known in school for her quick brain, but the solution to their problems burst upon her.

They were, after all, a squad. This was Angie's sister cheerleader. They cheered together — somehow they must triumph together. They could not be brought to shameful defeat, not when Angie was there to prevent it.

Angie stuck her slender ankle into the aisle. Hooking it around Mary Ellen's leg before Mary Ellen could begin to sense what was happening to

160

her balance, Angie kicked. Mary Ellen cried out, confused, falling, arms flailing as she tried to catch herself. She was much harder to knock over than the average girl: She practiced cheerleading hours every day.

Mary Ellen would have struck her head cruelly against the sharp corner of the display case if Angie hadn't blocked her fall with her body. "What the —" said Mary Ellen thickly.

The saleswoman was speaking much louder, however. "The hat!" she was crying.

Angie saw to her delight that she had completely crushed the silly purple hat. "Oh, I'm so sorry!" she said instantly. "It's ruined. I will pay for it, of course. Don't worry about a thing. It's all my clumsy fault, anyway."

Angie stood up, half knocking Mary Ellen back to the ground.

"Perhaps the hat can be put back in shape," said Angie brightly. "Let's go over to the counter and see." She jostled the saleswoman, who rather irritably let herself be herded toward the counter.

Angie did not look behind her. Whatever tangle Mary Ellen was in, let Pres handle it — although Pres definitely did not appear to be up to this particular occasion. Party boy, Angie thought to herself. You handle the dates and the dances; I'll handle the crimes.

She almost laughed. She kept up a running chat with the saleswoman on the best way to handle the crushed brim of the hat. Angie's hand slid down into Mary Ellen's purse, which she had deftly taken when she knocked Mary Ellen down, trying to locate the earrings by feeling for them. They were still on top. Angie's fingers closed around them and she drew them up to her face and cocked her head, looking at them admiringly. The saleswoman looked confused, as if she could not imagine where Angie had gotten those earrings.

Brightly, Angie said, "Aren't these lovely! You just have the loveliest things in this shop. But since I'm buying the hat, I guess I have to pass on the earrings, don't I?"

Her voice sounded false. But the saleswoman simply agreed that *two* major purchases were going to be tough. She wrote up the hat and then put the earrings gently back into the display case. If she had a flicker of suspicion, it was gone. Angie had saved Mary Ellen.

Mary Ellen, staggering to her feet — half furious and half embarrassed at being made to fall in public like that — turned just in time to see Angie's slender wrist disappear into *her*, Mary Ellen's, purse and bring out a pair of glittering gold earrings.

I'm going to throw up! Mary Ellen thought. She left Marnie's trembling. Pres Tilford, who also felt as if he might throw up, took her arm and led her to one of the redwood benches that wrapped in an octagon around a huge fern planter. Never in his entire life had Pres felt so unequal to an occasion. Mary Ellen? he kept thinking, stunned. It's true? It's really *true*.

Angie came out of Marnie's, wearing the purple hat. "It's okay, Mary Ellen," said Angie proudly. "I fixed it."

Mary Ellen could not speak.

Nancy came out of the store more confused than anybody. "What is going on?" she said. "Vanessa just fled from the shopping mall."

"What do you mean?" said Pres.

"*Vanessa!* That rotten, stinking, nasty Vanessa!"

All three cheerleaders stared at Angie. Angie *never* said bad things about other people.

"She slipped those earrings right into Mary Ellen's purse," Angie said. "I saw her do it. It was deliberate. It was no mistake. And then she began walking over to the saleslady in the back of the shop, and I knew she was going to tell her she'd seen Mary Ellen shoplift. That girl isn't just nasty, she's *evil!*"

Thank God I didn't say a single word, Pres thought. I thought Angie saved Mary Ellen from getting *caught*, not from getting framed. Relief at not having said anything against Mary Ellen — whom after all, he had kissed and held many times — swamped Pres.

Nancy said, "That cheat book. . . . She must have done that, too."

Angie gasped. "How did you know about that?"

"I found it in your purse that night at my party, when I was looking for your new lipstick or nail polish or whatever. I nearly died. Because

163

it supported the rumor that you were cheating."

Four cheerleaders exchanged shudders of disbelief.

"It sounds like — what do they call it in television cop series? — her *modus operandi*," said Pres. "Start rumor. Make rumor more vicious. Supply evidence by dropping it into purse."

"I think we should kill her," said Nancy.

"So do I," said Angie, the angel of Tarenton. "If you could have seen Vanessa's expression when she put those earrings into Mary Ellen's purse! She enjoyed it. She loved thinking about Mary Ellen getting into terrible trouble."

"Criminal charges," said Mary Ellen thinly. "It was bad enough to have to put up with those horrible, awful rumors. But there would have been policemen questioning me."

"Arresting you," said Pres, squeezing her again. He was not sure if this was for his own reassurance or hers. "Because you would have had the evidence *on* you."

"What is the matter with this group?" Walt's cheerful voice asked. "I leave you guys planning to wander through Marnie's trying on hats and I come back to tears on cheeks, trembling chins, furious faces, and jelly legs."

"Oh, Walt!" Angie cried. "You just won't believe what happened in there!" She told him every detail, with the other cheerleaders adding their interpretations.

"And I think," Nancy said, wrapping up, "that we should *kill* Vanessa."

Mary Ellen mostly listened, tears blurring her

vision. They *were* her team. They *had* stuck by her. They had even saved her.

"Homicide is also a crime," Walt pointed out. "I think we have to stop short of killing Vanessa."

"And now that I think about it," Mary Ellen said slowly, "it won't be easy to pin much on her. We have only Angie's word for the earrings getting into my purse that way. Now the earrings, the evidence, are back on the shelf. And the cheat book Nancy saw in Angie's purse *we're* sure Vanessa made up, but we can't prove it."

"Nobody ever proved the source of a rumor," Nancy added. Nancy sat down on Mary Ellen's other side. "You're white as a sheet. Try to calm down. I know it's terrible, but you're okay now." Nancy looked up at Angie, who was still too mad to sit down. "Do you think Vanessa definitely understood that you saw her?"

"Oh, yes! She panicked and ran. I guess she thought I was going to turn *her* in."

Pres said, "I could run Vanessa over with my Porsche."

"What?" Mary Ellen said. "And get blood all over the finish?"

They laughed. Reaching out hands the way they did in the Dynamite cheer, Pres, Mary Ellen, Nancy, Walt, and Angie formed a circle of linked fingers. Olivia's absence was noticeable because they were off balance. But they were so happy, so relieved that this terrible episode had been solved with nobody on the cheerleading squad damaged beyond repair, that they kept on laughing, hugging, and embracing.

Walt said, "I think it's time for that ice cream."

"We can talk over what to do to Vanessa there," Nancy agreed. "Come on, everybody: My treat."

Very casually, Pres said, "By the way, Mary Ellen, just out of curiosity, how *did* you earn the money to buy the stuff you've gotten lately?"

Mary Ellen flushed. "I've been doing laundry twice a week for my neighbors," she said.

"Oh, is *that* all," Pres said. "Well, better keep that to yourself. Ardith wouldn't like it."

It was a stupid secret, Mary Ellen thought. If I'd thrown pride away and admitted from the beginning where the money came from, the rumor could never have taken hold. Mary Ellen looked at Angie, her saviour, wearing the crazy purple hat at such a rakish angle. "I need to pay you back for the hat," she said. "That's my responsibility."

Angie shook her head vigorously. "I love this hat. This is me, Angie, the successful sleuth. Call me Nancy Drew in this hat."

Nancy Drew led the way into the Farm Shop. Troy was still sitting in the first booth with his new girl. Mary Ellen looked at him and found it did not hurt her at all anymore that he had so quickly replaced her. He was not much of a person after all. He had not stood by her.

Rescued twice in one week. First by Patrick. Now the squad.

Oh, *friends,* Mary Ellen thought gladly. Thank God for friends.

CHAPTER

12

It was an away basketball game.

Ardith gathered her Varsity squad in front of her. How splendid they looked in their bright scarlet and pristine white! Blonde hair and brown curls, slim legs and muscular shoulders. Truly, she had the finest six girls and boys Tarenton could offer!

And what proof of that in the last few days! Ardith shuddered, thinking of all she had been through. "You did the right thing to tell me about Vanessa," she said. "I admire you for not going after her yourselves. Not many adults could be so restrained. I've had conferences with Mrs. Oetjen, with Dr. Barlow, and with Vanessa."

"Oh, good," Angie said. "She's going to a reformatory."

"She's not going anywhere," Mrs. Engborg said. "Without proof and more witnesses, there isn't much we can actually *do* to Vanessa."

"Especially when Daddy is the superintendent of schools and won't believe anything bad about his perfect daughter," Olivia put in.

The coach did not deny this.

"*We* could frame *her*," Olivia suggested.

Mary Ellen shivered. "Don't even *think* such a thing. It's too terrible. I know. I was there."

The coach said, "However, I think we can be sure that no more trouble will come from Vanessa. She was thoroughly frightened by how close she came to being caught, and she knows that we know."

"I wish I'd heard that talk," Angie said. "I wish I'd been a fly on the wall when you interrogated her."

Walt began laughing. "We're going to have to watch you, Angie. Now that you think you're Nancy Drew, you might bug the locker rooms so you can listen to conversations of criminal intent."

"Nothing criminal happens in locker rooms," Olivia said. "All she'd get on tape is the sound of sweat pouring off skin. You know what I resent most in all this, though?"

"No. What?" they asked her.

"I missed it! All the action took place when I was off with Michael!"

"I bet not *all* the action was at the mall," Mary Ellen said. "I bet *some* of the action was between you and Michael."

Olivia blushed.

Ardith Engborg let them tease each other for a few more minutes. How wonderful to have a

168

normal squad of teenagers back again! "All right, kids," she said. "Time. Mary Ellen, you have your cheer roster ready? You know what you're doing?"

"Mrs. Engborg," Mary Ellen said in a drawl, "I *always* know what I'm doing."

The kids laughed again. Getting in line prior to running out on the basketball court, they jostled each other happily. Angie put the garish shapeless purple hat on her dark hair and made silly faces from under its lopsided brim.

"Angie!" the coach cried. "Take that horrible headgear off *now!*"

"Please let me wear it," Angie begged. "It's a symbol. It's triumph. It's victory."

Ardith snatched the hat from her head. "Tarenton colors," she said severely, "are red and white. Not a drop of purple. Behave yourself, Angie."

The coach put the hat on her own head. Tiny blonde Ardith Engborg, wearing blue jeans, a white blouse, and red sweater tied over her shoulders — topped with a crazy purple hat. "*I'll* wear the Nancy Drew symbol," she said loftily. She gave Mary Ellen a light push and six Varsity members ran out on the court, their laughter genuine, their teamwork real.

Across from them sat the Tarenton faithful, who'd come by fan bus and private car to an away game. For the fans, those snowy white and splashy scarlet uniforms meant pride and spirit. They began clapping even before Mary Ellen did.

Mary Ellen gauged the place where she wanted to stand. Each cheerleader stopped exactly two paces apart. Their kicks were high, their steps in perfect order.

Directly opposite Mary Ellen sat Patrick. He raised an arm in a victory salute and Mary Ellen gave him her biggest smile. He had helped her when she needed it; he always did. She wanted to keep him close to her, but not let him think she was going to be his girl. Pres had seemed involved with her again, and there was a whole world of men out there.

In the second row, a flushed and pretty Kerry waved her fingers at Pres. He raised his eyebrows at her, but he remembered how Mary Ellen had felt when he had held her after the earrings bit . . . warm, compliant, sexy. Maybe he was just a playboy, not meant for one woman.

Angie and Walt faced the crowd, ready for the pure joy of cheering. Angie was delirious with relief, but she was also feeling something totally unlike Angie . . . a need to get back at Vanessa.

Mary Ellen turned sharply and faced her squad. "Ready?"

"Ready!" they cried, with an enthusiasm unmatched in their cheering history. Two hundred fans waited for them, ready to love them.

What happens when Nancy and Olivia fall for the same guy? Read Cheerleaders #4, FEUDING.